BOSTON PLAYER

MELISSA BELLE

Autumn Ink Press

ALSO BY MELISSA BELLE

JARED

LIAM

Bonus Wild Men Stories

WILD MAN (Colton and Sky prequel novella)

WILD VALENTINE (Ayden and Bella short story)

Sign up for Melissa's Newsletter to get a free story and to receive alerts and updates on upcoming book releases.

To March in Paris

ABOUT

He was her first. And she wants him to be her last.

Brooklyn

When I knew him, Duncan was a soccer star.

But to me, he was my first love. My only love.

Six years ago, he was the boy with the midnight dark hair and impossibly gray-blue eyes I met one summer in Europe. When the world felt dark, Duncan was my light. He kissed me, cared for me, and protected me. And then I went home, and he stayed in Europe to pursue his dreams.

I followed my dreams by going to college. And the years passed. Duncan never left my heart, but I didn't expect to see him again.

Because first loves aren't meant to last...

Duncan

I was supposed to stay away from Brooklyn.

She was too young, too good, and she was only in Paris for a short while.

But she got under my skin right away—that brilliant, sassy blonde with the killer smile and long, tanned legs.

She twisted my heart into knots and made me want to stay in her arms forever rather than chase my dream. She was like lightning in a bottle—I was sure when she left Paris, I'd missed my chance with her for good.

For six years, I was right. Until I agree to take part in a charity soccer game in Boston and a gorgeous blonde with tanned legs runs onto the field to see her cousins who turn out to be three of my closest friends.

So Brooklyn is back in my life...but her cousins have warned me off her. She's like their baby sister and they don't want to see her hurt.

I don't want to break the bro code.

But time is short. And the fire between Brooklyn and me stills burns.

And I'm not giving Brooklyn up again...for anyone.

PROLOGUE

Six Years Earlier...
  Paris, France
  Brooklyn
  I've been living in Paris for a month already, soaking up the culture and the cafés. And attending a sporting event wasn't high on my list of priorities.

  But then I found a game on television and saw what the players look like.

  How do you say hot in French?

  Beau.

  Tres beau.

  My cousins back in Boston adore soccer and they made me promise to attend at least one game.

  "And get a damn picture to prove you were there," my oldest cousin, Ryder, had grumbled.

  So here I am. Staring out at the soccer field. I'm sorry— the pitch as Europeans call it. I don't think I'll be able to get used to that. What I am getting used to, as an American living in France, is all of the mistakes I make on a daily basis.

  So watching a club game for younger players, the ones

who hope to make it big someday, but aren't there yet, seems safe enough. The stands aren't packed and I'm able to get a front row seat.

But I can't see well enough. The ball is a damn blur and I can't tell who the hell has it.

So I stand up and make my way down to the field, sorry —*the pitch*—making sure to stay on the sideline and far away from the team benches. And then I put my full attention on the players.

Number thirteen in particular.

Midnight hair and a lean, muscled body, he moves lethally across the field like a panther about to strike.

I'm enchanted by him, and I step ever closer to the edge of the playing field.

Too close, apparently, because I'm suddenly yanked backward.

"Fais attention!" A security guard snaps at me.

"Pardon," I say with a nod.

But I can't take my eyes off number thirteen.

Which just happens to be my lucky number. Yes, I go against type.

He has the ball, and he's coming closer.

And closer.

He races past me so close that I jump as he maneuvers around a defender and effortlessly keeps the ball in his possession. He suddenly turns and sends a perfect pass toward a streaking teammate, who scores just as the referee blows the whistle to announce the halftime.

I jump up and down screaming in excitement as the players start to head off the field in the opposite direction of where I'm standing. But number thirteen jogs in my direction.

Right toward me.

I don't have time to react before he easily lifts me off the ground with one strong arm and walks with me until we're a good twenty feet back from the edge of the pitch.

I remain in his hot, sweaty arms, my face pressed against his chest. I can hear his heart beating fast, and I hope he can't hear mine because unlike the way he's been exerting himself all game, I have no reason to have an elevated pulse.

"Hey." He puts me down and smiles at me.

And oh my Lord, I nearly fan myself.

Because this boy...he has the most beautiful smile I've ever seen in my eighteen years.

"Tu dois etre prudent."

Be careful.

"Right. I know. I'm sorry."

But I don't want to be careful right now. I want to be reckless and wild and to stay in his arms.

His gray-blue eyes widen. "You're American."

"Yes."

"Me too."

"Really?" I smile at him. "Where are you from?"

"New York. What about you?"

"I grew up in suburban Massachusetts, but I'm moving to Boston at the end of the summer."

"You're in Paris for a while?"

I nod.

His smile widens, and he reaches for the phone in my hand. "If I give you my number, will you call me tonight?"

That would be a hell yes.

And for the next thirty-three days, Duncan Hyde and I were inseparable.

Until the day I left Paris to go back to reality.

"You're going to be a big soccer star," I whispered to Duncan as he kissed me goodbye in the morning dew of the Paris dawn. "I'll be wishing the best for you forever."

His lips lingered on mine. "Do you want me to come with you?"

I shook my head. "Are you kidding me? This is your dream. Go after it. Besides, I'm only eighteen. My cousins would kill you if we ran away together."

"They'd have to find us first," Duncan said teasingly, his gray-blue eyes belying the sadness he was trying to hide.

"True."

He pulled me into his arms. "You deserve to go big too, Brooklyn. Promise me you will."

"I promise."

CHAPTER ONE

Brooklyn

The Manhattan sky is dark and threatening as I leave my high-rise apartment building for the last time. Dragging two suitcases behind me, I walk to the curb and raise my hand.

When a cab pulls up, I wait while he deposits my bags in the trunk, and then I climb into the back seat.

"Where to?" he asks as he gets into the driver's seat.

"JFK Airport."

I twist my long hair up into a messy knot on the top of my head and flick through my phone while the cab driver weaves through the gridlock of Manhattan traffic. My cousins texted me three times, wanting to know what time my flight arrives. First Ryder, then Emmett, and then Killian. Always in that order, and always because they care about me and know they're the only family I've got left. Yes, I've also got Ronen and Shane and the rest of the O'Shea clan, but Ryder, Emmett, and Killian are the only ones I knew growing up. They're the cousins who were there for me when I lost it all. The ones who took me in and helped raise me when I had no one else left.

I text them back the time and then I rest my head against the seat and stare out at the cityscape passing by in a whirl.

Heading home to Massachusetts is bringing up memories I've tried hard to forget. Sad memories of loss, but also a reminder of what came before I moved in with the O'Shea brothers in Boston. My one and only time living out of the country. The one and only time I fell in love.

I let out a heavy sigh and stare out at the colorless city of Manhattan. I got my college degree. I even landed my dream job.

And I did it all on my own. The decision to break up with my first love was the right decision.

So why do I feel so lonely?

CHAPTER TWO

Duncan

Bucca's kitchen is busy and bustling as I bring in the last customers' empty plates. The tiramisu I made went over well, and I'm not working the dinnertime rush, so I set out the ingredients for a new batch and spend the next hour preparing it. Once that's done, I take off my apron and grab my bag. I love the energy of Boston's North End, especially at mealtime, but I'm ready for some time off.

"Quitting time, D," I say to my cousin, Diego.

He takes off his chef's hat and grins at me. "Are you ready for today's charity game? All ticket and concession proceeds go to the foster kids organization Roberto partnered with."

"I was born ready," I say back.

I'm only half-kidding. Soccer's in my blood. My mom played in high school, and it's the one thing she passed down to me that I actually appreciate.

"Let's go," he says. "Caleb and the O'Shea's are meeting us there."

As we step outside Bucca's Ristorante, I glance up as a plane flies overhead toward Logan Airport.

And maybe it's because I'm about to go play soccer, or maybe it's the warm afternoon, unusually humid for Boston in November, but my mind is brought back to Paris, France seven years ago and a blonde with a killer smile who took my breath away and stole my heart all in the same moment. No one else has gotten inside me since. No one else has made it past a few nights.

I shake my head to clear the memories.

That girl, and that time in my life, are long gone.

———

The Boston sky is blue and cloudless as I dribble the soccer ball down the left side of the field.

"Cut!" I yell to Diego.

He's not a soccer player, but he does what I say, and I cross the ball to him in perfect rhythm to match his stride. All he has to do is tap the ball and it's a goal for Bucca's Ristorante. Between that and my two earlier goals, we're up three to nothing on the team sponsored by O'Shea's Bar. The small crowd of mostly family and friends, plus a few busloads of foster kids, cheer, and I slap Diego's hand.

Killian O'Shea and his older brother, Ryder, meet us in the middle of the field with Ronen and we all shake hands.

"These charity games are a good chance for you to show off, Duncan," Killian says to me. "Shit, you're good."

I used to be good, but that feels like a long time ago.

"Sucks about your knee," Ronen says with a shake of his head.

It does.

After tearing up my knee, I lost my sponsors. I had to give up on the European leagues and head home with no back-up plan. The good news is my knee doesn't stop me from exercising. I just can't train the way a professional would need to.

And until these charity games were organized last month, I hadn't played soccer. Not since I moved to Boston to work alongside Roberto, my biological father and Diego's uncle, at Roberto's family restaurant. Working at Bucca's Ristorante has been amazing. Doesn't mean I don't miss the hell out of playing soccer.

The game keeps going and soon I have the ball in my possession again.

I cut hard to shake off my defender, but he stays with me. I'm able to outrun him and then I hit a perfect pass to Caleb Walker, my future brother-in-law.

He kicks the ball back to me but his pass is off-target, and I have to shift to control it with my thigh before I strike it mid-air in an arc toward the right side of the net.

It lobs in easily.

End of game.

Amidst the cheers of the crowd, I stop and toss the soccer ball to one of the foster kids watching us on the sidelines.

"That's how you make sure you keep possession," I explain. "Don't give up on the ball until you know what you're going to do with it, and stay available so it can come back to you."

The kid nods. "Yes, Mr. Sorelli."

"What's your name?" I ask him.

"Tim."

"Nice to meet you, Tim." I lift my shirt and use the hem to wipe the sweat off my brow. My dark hair is sticking to my head. "Call me Duncan," I tell Tim. "Mister makes me feel old."

"That's because you are old," Diego calls over to me.

I flip him off before I head over to where Killian and his brothers Ryder and Emmett are standing with Diego, Caleb, and Ronen in the middle of the field.

"I'm younger than you are," I say to Diego.

"Hey, age is just a number." Ryder runs a hand through his dark hair and smirks. "Turning thirty's not all bad."

Emmett's blue eyes crinkle as he smirks. "My cousin likes to remind everyone of that fact."

Ronen laughs, his eyes brightening with amusement. "You're nearly as old as him. Besides, getting old is a good thing. It means we're still here and breathing."

True. And I know how lucky I am. To have a group of people who have my back, all because I found my birth certificate that my mom had buried under piles of stuff in the spare closet. Moving to Boston with my twin, Starr, changed my life. I connected with my father and his entire family including Diego, and I've also gotten close with Caleb and the O'Shea brothers.

I was never a foster kid, but I was lost and alone, and my mom was too busy trying to climb the Manhattan social ladder to worry much about Starr and me. Not having parents who fully get behind you can be tough, and I'd like to help any kid who needs it.

So when my dad asked Diego and I if we wanted to participate in his sponsoring a team for charity and he suggested soccer, I didn't hesitate.

"And you're getting married soon," I say to Caleb. "Lot to look forward to."

"Can't wait," he says, and I know he means it. My half-sister, Paris, and Caleb are head over heels for each other.

I glance up and my gaze snags on a blonde making her way down to the field. My heart drops into my gut as I watch her walk.

God, she looks so familiar, so much like...

What the fuck am I even saying?

You're playing mind games, Duncan. Get a fucking grip.

I turn away from the blonde and try to refocus on whatever the hell Diego's joking about.

Returning to the world of soccer, even in this lighthearted capacity, is bringing back memories I thought I'd permanently pushed away.

But that's all they are...memories.

"Hey there, O'Shea boys!"

The strikingly-familiar tone of her voice jerks me out of my thoughts. I turn toward the voice, and Killian's face splits into a wide grin as the woman, wearing skinny jeans and a pink Boston hoodie with the words O'Shea's Bar on it, flies across the field and into his arms.

I freeze as I realize why I was mesmerized by the blonde in the stands just moments ago.

She's now standing across from me—*and she's the girl from my past.*

Brooklyn Carter.

I swallow as Killian hugs her hard. Ryder and Emmett are next. Both guys pick her up like she's the most important person in their life before she wriggles free with a laugh and then hugs Ronen. Ryder throws his arm around her as she turns to face us.

"This is our baby cousin, Brookie O'Shea. She's taking a well-earned vacation and visiting from New York this week. Hopefully longer."

Brookie O'Shea. I only knew her as Brooklyn, and she definitely went by Brooklyn Carter in Paris. So why the name change?

"Brooklyn," she says with an eye roll at the O'Shea brothers. "They think I'm still six years old."

Caleb and Diego both say hello to her as Killian introduces all three of us.

But Brooklyn's hazel eyes fix on me, and I see the shock

cross her face before she shutters her expression. "I know you."

"And I know you."

She keeps her gaze on me. "Sorelli, huh? What happened to Hyde?"

"Found my father," I say.

"Wow." She smiles genuinely. "That's wonderful."

"It is." I don't want to hug her when I'm all sweaty like this, so I lean forward and lightly kiss her cheek. She smells like daisies, and I don't miss the sharp inhale of her breath as my lips touch her soft skin. Her long blond hair hangs past her shoulders, and a lock of it brushes my jaw as I kiss her cheek.

Electricity zings through me, and I freeze, my mouth touching her smooth skin.

Knowing all eyes are on us, especially her cousins', I step back and flash what I hope is a casual smile. "Good to see you, Brooklyn. It's been a long time."

Brooklyn's still gorgeous with long legs and curves everywhere. She's also a woman now. Last time I saw her, she was still growing up, something we did together.

"Nice to see you also, Duncan." Her tone is also casual, and I'm probably the only one who hears the bite of pain. "Are you living in Boston now? My cousins never mentioned you."

Killian looks between Brooklyn and me with a hard look in his eyes.

"Why would I mention him? How the hell do you two know each other?"

"When I was playing soccer over in Europe," I say. "Your cousin and I met at a game."

"And?" Emmett asks. "Then what?"

Brooklyn flings her hand in the air toward Emmett. "And nothing. We hung out in rated G, group settings that summer until I moved in with you overprotective cousins of mine who might as well be my big brothers for how you're behaving right now."

"We are like your big brothers," Ryder says. "And Duncan isn't the right guy for you."

"Oh really?" Brooklyn says with her hands on her hips. "Why is that?"

"Because he's a player," Killian answers her. "He's probably dated every single woman in the Bay State."

"And you think that would bother me?" Brooklyn says sharply. "You don't know what I'm looking for. Maybe I want a fling with a hot player."

My senses are on high alert, and Brooklyn's temper is just making me more affected by her than I already was. She's gorgeous with eyes blazing as she glares at her three cousins. Their anger, however, is directed solely at me.

"Stay away from her," Killian says to me in a don't-fuck-with-me tone. "I mean it."

I put my hands up in a surrender gesture. "Don't come after me, O'Shea. I didn't even know you guys then."

"But you know us now, right?" Ryder asks me, his blue eyes laser focused.

The O'Shea family isn't exactly known for following the straight and narrow. The brothers are always on the right side of the law, though. But they are definitely rough around the edges and I personally wouldn't want to cross them.

That doesn't mean I don't think Brooklyn's worth the risk.

Because for that one summer in Paris, Brooklyn and I got to know each other quite well. We spent nearly every night together. And I'm not sure I'm over her yet.

"All you handsome Boston boys," Brooklyn says teasingly to the group of us, but her gaze lingers on me. "I'm happy to be home."

"How are you?" I ask her softly.

"I'm good," she says. "I've been working as a financial analyst for a Manhattan advertising firm."

"Good for you," I say. "I remember you were planning to go into finance."

The others fade away as Brooklyn and I stare at each other.

Killian's grip around his cousin's shoulders tightens and he shoots me another pointed look. "Okay, let's go. See you guys later."

I turn my head to watch the five O'Shea's as they walk away.

"Hey. Put your tongue back in your damn mouth." Diego shoots me a look. "You think the O'Shea brothers are going to take kindly to you hitting on their baby cousin?"

No, I'm sure they're not. I'm also not sure I care.

"Diego's right." Caleb shakes his head at me warningly. "You've got your pick of any woman in the city. Best to stay away from Brooklyn O'Shea."

"I'll try," I say.

And I mean it.

Until Brooklyn turns her head and looks back at me over her shoulder. She shoots me a dazzling smile, the kind she used to show only to me. And I nearly drop to my knees.

I wave back at her, no longer sure I can keep my promise.
And no longer sure I want to.

CHAPTER THREE

Brooklyn

"The guy you fell for in Europe lives in Boston?" My best friend, Miranda, and her identical twin sister, Stella, speak in unison like they often do. "The same one we met when we visited you? How long has he been here?"

"I don't know any of the details yet. But I'm going to find out." I sigh. "I don't get it. He was sooo good at soccer. So why didn't he turn pro like he wanted to?"

I blow out a breath as I stretch out in the booth across from them at O'Shea's Bar. Only one booth in the entire bar, and we always take it. Miranda and Stella never come to this bar unless I'm in town. Like me, they grew up in suburbia. They moved to Boston after college, but don't go out to bars or clubs often. They prefer to hang out in the coffee shop that they co-own and get their highs off of caffeine.

Right now, however, the three of us are good and buzzed, a tradition we've kept up at least one time whenever I come home to visit. We eat burgers and fries, have a few tequila shots, and then shift to cheap beer. My ice blue spaghetti-strap tank and faded jeans are better suited to summer weather, but I've been hot since I ran into Duncan earlier today.

"God." I bury my face in my hands. "I thought I'd never see him again. I was sooo sure."

It wasn't personal. It was more about wanting to leave the past where it belongs than any negative feelings. Duncan was there for me when I had no one, and what we shared are some of my most treasured memories. But memories aren't usually meant to be resurrected.

Although in the deepest recesses of my heart, I think I'm afraid.

As a girl who's not new to loss, the potential of losing Duncan for a second time is crushing. I preferred to keep him in my rearview—a beautiful sunset I can look back at and admire, but not anything I have to worry about breaking my heart.

But now, he's here in Boston. And so am I.

God. Why didn't any of my cousins ever mention Duncan's former last name? Did they even know it?

I glance up at the bar. Emmett's running the place himself at the moment, which is good news for me because with only one O'Shea in the house, he can't take time away from business to focus on his baby cousin. He, Ryder, and Killian spent the entire way home from the game grilling me about Duncan and how close we got in France six years ago. Of course, I didn't give them any details.

"Brooklyn."

"Yeah," I say in a monotone, barely registering that Stella's speaking to me.

"You still wear the ring Duncan gave you around your neck," she points out.

I jerk my head up. "I don't always wear it," I say defensively.

She reaches for my neckline. Before I can stop her, she's

pulled down my scoop neck to reveal the simple gold band on a linked chain dangling right between my bra cups.

I jerk back from her. "No grabsies."

"Looks like a wedding band, you know." Stella stares at me, unblinking.

"It wasn't! It was more like...a kind of promise ring," I say. "But not the kind where we promised to stay together. We didn't have that kind of relationship. It was different than that."

The ring was Duncan's goodbye gift to remind me of what we shared. Of what we gave to each other. It was a promise to each other to "go big" in our lives by chasing our dreams and not giving up no matter the obstacles. I wear the ring to remind myself to stay strong. Earning my college degree, getting a job in New York City and fighting to move up the ladder in my field—none of that came easily to a girl who had no one but her cousins left for family.

"Whatever the meaning of the ring, you clearly never got over him," Miranda says in a clinical tone. She shoves her glasses up her nose. "So think of this as God's gift to you. This time, you're going to get over Duncan Hyde once and for all."

"Duncan Sorelli," I say automatically.

"Sorelli," she repeats.

"How do you propose she does that?" Stella asks.

"You fuck him."

Stella and I stare at Miranda. It's unlike her to speak so crudely.

"What?" I say. "How would that help me get over him?"

"You've both grown up since you left Paris. That was years ago. Now, you're both adults. You won't be swayed by good sex. And you'll probably find that the sex isn't even as good as you remembered."

Remembering Duncan's hard body and wicked grin today on the football field, I highly doubt that.

But I let Miranda continue her theory. "Set terms with him first. Say you'd like to try to reconnect for a week. After this time of not-so-amazing sex is over, you'll realize you're over him as well." She raises her bottle of beer. "Mission accomplished."

I open my mouth to answer her, but all thoughts leave my head when the door opens and Duncan strolls into the bar with Killian, Ryder, and the other guys I met earlier, Diego and Caleb. Diego and Caleb are each with a woman.

All the guys have great bodies and none of them are lacking in confidence. The women are both gorgeous and chatting animatedly to one another. The entire group strides through the bar like they own it, with Diego laughing at something Caleb's saying. My gaze stays on Duncan as they all head toward Emmett behind the bar.

"There he is!" I whisper.

Stella whips her head around so fast her hair flies off her shoulders. "Oh, my."

"Right?" I lose sight of Duncan in the crowd and shift my gaze over to Stella. "He's..."

"Filled out," she says as she turns back to me. "Grown up. Muscles everywhere."

Miranda doesn't turn around. She just rolls her eyes at us both. "You two are hopeless."

"We are not!" Stella says defensively. "He's gorgeous—you should see him!"

Miranda scoffs. "Stella, you'd think any guy was hot. I'm sure Duncan is no more handsome or sexy than the next man."

"Oh, really?"

I look over Miranda's shoulder at the broad-shouldered,

dark-haired man with magnificent gray-blue eyes that are currently swimming with humor.

"Duncan," I say in a husky tone I don't recognize. I clear my throat and try again. "Hey."

Miranda and Stella's long, brunette hair flies off their backs as they whip their heads around.

"Oh. My." Miranda's gaze travels from Duncan's face all the way down his body. By the time her eyes return to his face, she's full-on blushing. "You've grown up nice," she says in a tone filled with begrudging admiration.

"Thanks, Miranda. Nice to see you again. Stella, you too." He steps forward and eases himself into my side of the booth. "Hey, Brooklyn. Two times in one day, huh?"

I wink at him. "Fate?"

He leans closer and raises his eyebrows. "Thought you didn't believe in fate."

"I don't," I say. "But you do."

"Sometimes," he says. "When I can't explain something any other way."

He says the comment casually, but his hand goes to my thigh. He brushes my leg briefly, just long enough for me to bite down on my lip to suppress a moan.

Across from me, Miranda's eyes narrow on the Formica like she can see through it to my thigh underneath.

Stella clears her throat. "So! Duncan. How did your life turn out? Did you make it big?"

I laugh at how she unwittingly says the same phrase he and I used to swear by.

Next to me, he chuckles like he knows what I'm thinking.

"I'm happy, yes. Blew out my knee over in Europe so I had to quit soccer..."

"Oh, I'm so sorry," I say softly, my chest aching for him.

"I appreciate that," he says softly. "But that's in the past. I work at my father's Italian restaurant and I'm enjoying learning how to run a business."

"Well, that's exciting," Stella says sincerely. "Congratulations."

"Thanks." His cheeks flush like he's embarrassed by the praise.

And my heart, which could never stay guarded against Duncan Hyde now Sorelli, opens even more. "You should be proud of yourself," I tell him. "You did good."

He shifts his gaze directly to me. "I thought of you often. You know that, right?"

Okay, my heart is now fully engaged. "Not exactly," I murmur.

"It's true." He brushes one of my hairs off of my forehead and tucks it back behind my ear.

Miranda, who seems to have rediscovered her armor, glares at us both. "You two need to get a room."

"Why the glare? I thought that was what you wanted us to do, Miranda." I blame that slip of the tongue on the tequila shots the three of us had before we moved on to beer.

Beside me, Duncan flinches. "What am I missing?" he says.

"A lot." Miranda puts her statement on hold while she downs the rest of her beer. She slams the empty bottle onto the Formica and stands up. "Come on, Stella. These two need to catch up."

CHAPTER FOUR

Duncan

"What was that about?" I ask Brooklyn once we're alone.

She hesitates.

I wait patiently. I know Brooklyn. She's never been the type to keep silent. Sure enough—

"She thinks I need to fuck you out of my system."

I spit out the sip of beer I just took.

"What?" I finally say. "Why would she say that?"

Brooklyn shrugs. "She's drunk."

"Brooklyn..."

I'm cut off by the arrival of Diego and Caleb at our booth.

"Hey." They sit opposite us where Stella and Miranda just vacated.

Diego smiles at Brooklyn. "Brooklyn, right?"

He doesn't say it in a flirtatious way, just in his usual friendly Diego way. But I don't want anyone interrupting my time with Brooklyn right now. I've waited years to see her again, and I'm going to make the most of it.

"Where's your fiancé?" I say to Caleb. "And your girl-friend?" I ask Diego.

"Up at the bar."

I shove a wad of bills at Caleb. "Why don't you two go join them and get us a round of drinks?"

Caleb looks between Brooklyn and me.

He doesn't say anything, though; he just grabs Diego's arm and they head to the bar.

"I have a better idea than Miranda's," I say as if we were never interrupted.

"What's that?" Brooklyn's cheeks are adorably pink like she's just realizing how blunt her comment was.

"A date."

"A date?" She stares at me, her eyes wide.

And if I'm not mistaken, panicked.

"What's so crazy about that?" I ask her.

"You and I broke up, for one."

"So? We didn't break up because we stopped wanting to be together."

"I know, but..." She looks at me. "My cousins are as protective as ever. You saw how Killian threatened you."

"You think Killian scares me?"

She scoffs. "I don't think anyone has ever scared you. But I don't want to come between you and your friends."

"Don't worry about me. I can take care of myself. And you're a woman now. Not a teenager. They can't stop us."

"They can try." She laughs. "And Kil said you live upstairs in the apartment next door to the three of them? You do realize I'm crashing with them, right? I mean, seriously, could you live any closer to them?"

"Hey, at least we aren't housemates."

"True." Her eyes sparkle. "They can't kill you from outside the door."

"A door and plenty of brick in between," I joke.

———

Brooklyn

God, Duncan's still so easy to talk to. No other guy has ever gotten my sense of humor like he did. I forgot how much I missed this—bantering with him about anything and everything. And the longer I look at him, the more I want to get to know him all over again.

"So when do you propose we go on this date?" I ask him. "You're pretty busy with the restaurant, I'm sure."

"You're only in town for a week, so I say we have that date right now." He tilts his head toward the door. "Let's go."

"Now? But I'm..." *Not ready.* "Out with the girls."

Like she heard me, Miranda pops into our personal space. "Take her wherever you want. We'll catch up tomorrow, Brooklyn."

"I hate you," I whisper as Duncan steps a few feet away. "I'm not going to sleep with him. Guaranteed."

"Uh-huh." Miranda smirks in amusement.

"And what about my cousins?" I glance toward the bar where Killian and Ryder are racing around filling customers' orders. I don't see Emmett, which means he's in the back room dealing with a delivery.

"Perfect time to leave," Miranda says, reading my mind. "They can't see the door from the bar, and if they ask, I'll say you were tired and went up to bed."

I may be staying with my cousins, but they have a guest room with its own private entrance that used to belong to their late father. So technically, I should be able to sneak in whenever I want to, and all three guys will no doubt be working the bar long past midnight.

"Or better yet," she says like she's thinking all this up in real time. "Why don't you text Killian that you're staying over my place?"

"I guess I could do that. Then the guys wouldn't worry."

"So do that. Stella and I want to get out of here anyway.

Now go," Miranda says. "Stop denying all the chemistry that's obviously still there. Even I can see it, and I'm a callous bitch. You've nearly got me turned on."

I spin on my heel and walk past Duncan.

"I'm ready," I say as I shoot off a text to Killian.

Duncan reaches me as I'm pushing open the door.

"Are you hungry?" he asks as he holds the door open for me to walk through.

"Starved. I didn't get dinner," I admit. "You?"

"I'm always up for a meal." He glances around. "We're only a few blocks from a hole-in-the-wall burrito place. I know how much you love Mexican food."

"You remember that?"

"Brooklyn." He searches my gaze. "Of course I remember."

I shrug, feeling my face heat. "It was a long time ago, Duncan."

"You know one of the things I've learned?" he says to me. "The most important memories tend to stick with me."

"What about the rest of your time in Europe?" I ask as I jump over the crack in the sidewalk. "How many beautiful women did you take out?"

"No one who meant anything to me." He waits until I pause in my sidewalk hopping and look up at him.

"You took loads of women out, didn't you?" I stick my tongue out at him. "Spare me the details."

He shakes his head. "The only woman I took to a nice hotel was my mom. She never would have come to see me play in Europe if she couldn't be pampered."

I know about his mom and his sister. I've never met them, but I know there's a lot of history and not all of it is positive.

Duncan stops outside a wooden door with a Burrito Café sign on it. He opens the door for us to enter.

Once we're seated and have ordered a burrito each plus

chips and guacamole, Duncan asks me, "So how has life been treating you?"

I give him a thumbs-up. "Much better than when we last saw each other. Back then you were the only bright spot in my summer." I pause. "I don't think I ever properly thanked you."

"You did," he assures me.

I fiddle with my napkin, my eyes down. "Losing my grandpa that summer was harder than I'd even imagined it would be."

Duncan's warm hand covers my own still clutching the napkin. "You handled it far better than most people would have. Your grandpa was the only parental figure you had left. Of course it was devastating. And you had to leave your hometown and move into a city you didn't know."

The night Grandpa died was my last in my childhood home. I was seventeen and had no one but my cousins to turn to. Emmett, Ryder, and Killian were going through their own struggles trying to figure out how to run their father's bar on their own. Mr. O'Shea had recently passed away also, and the four of us were like ships adrift at sea. My grandfather had stipulated in his will that I was to spend the first summer after he'd passed away in Paris with an old friend of his, Ms. Patty.

Ms. Patty was a wealthy, self-made woman who had never married, and she took me in reluctantly. She didn't pay me much attention while I was there, so I was free to do pretty much whatever I wanted in Paris, and once I met Duncan, I took full advantage of my freedom.

"I don't know that I handled it well." I continue to twist the napkin. "I'm not sure what I would have done if I hadn't met you. I mean, my French was abysmal!"

He chuckles. "You didn't need to speak French with me."

"Are you still multi-lingual?"

He nods. "I've added Italian now since I met my dad. I love it."

"Sorelli sounds like a good Italian name," I say. "What's your father like?"

"He's humble, hard-working, and loyal. Starr and I are lucky. And his entire family—his wife, Bianca and their daughter, Sophia, along with his other daughter, Paris and cousin Diego and his mom—they've all welcomed us in. Paris and Starr don't get along, but that's Starr's fault."

Duncan never liked to talk about his family, but he told me enough. I knew his twin sister had some issues and that his mom wasn't very nurturing.

"How is your mom?" I ask him quietly.

"She's the exact same." He rolls his shoulders. "Dating another wealthy businessman who doesn't look at her. And Starr...my sister could have used a better role model, let's just say that."

"Well, I'm so happy you found your dad."

"Me too."

His hand is still covering mine, and I fight the butterflies taking flight in my stomach.

"So-o-o." The word comes out stilted, and I clear my throat before continuing. "My cousins spent a good part of an hour warning me off of you."

Duncan's face is expressionless. "I don't blame them. They've got good reason to say that."

"You weren't a player when I knew you." I say it with certainty.

"You're right. I wasn't."

"So why the change?"

He swallows hard. "After my soccer dreams ended, I went into a dark place for a while. I was lost. And I turned to women. But I made sure to keep it casual so I couldn't get too close."

"So you couldn't get hurt the way your lost dream had hurt you," I surmise.

"Exactly."

"And you're still in that place?"

His eyes lock with mine. "I was never in that place with you, Brooklyn."

And...oh my. He just broke down some of my walls with that statement. Because I know Duncan. I know when he's telling the absolute truth and I know when he's dancing around it. Right now, his eyes are completely honest.

And if I'm being honest, I never stopped wanting him.

"So you're not in a relationship?" I dare to ask.

"No. You?"

I shake my head. "I'm quite single." I awkwardly withdraw my hand from his and start fiddling with my hair. "Which is probably good because I was transferred from my job in New York City."

"You were? The O'Shea's didn't mention that."

"I haven't told my cousins yet because you know how they are. They'll want to get way too involved in everything. Like where I should get an apartment, things like that. I love them, but they act like I'm still a kid sometimes."

"Are you moving away from the northeast?" Duncan asks me.

"No." I hesitate. "I'm coming home. To Boston."

Duncan's in the middle of taking a sip of water, and he chokes. Water flies out of his mouth and lands on the plastic red-and-white-checked tablecloth between us. He immediately wipes the water up with his napkin.

I bite back a smile. "I had no control over the where," I say truthfully. "I'm still working my way up in the world, so I don't exactly get a say in these things yet. And to be honest, I may look for a new job once I've settled in here. You can't tell now because I'm on vacation, but my job is non-stop, and now that I have it on my resume, I may look for a change."

"But you'll be living in Boston."

"Yes. That part is definite."

He runs a hand over his mouth. "Wow."

"Is that a good wow or a you-just-freaked-me-out wow?"

His gray-blue eyes twinkle. "That's an I-can't-fucking-believe-my-luck wow."

"Because we'll be in the same city again?" I ask him.

"Because...yes. And that means this week isn't the end of me getting to hang out with you." He shoots me a dazzling smile. "I think today should definitely be day one."

"Day one?"

"Of Duncan and Brooklyn. Part two."

I definitely had too much to drink at the bar, because I say, "Part one didn't end well for us. I don't think my heart could take another ending like that."

"What are you saying?"

"I'm saying..." I take advantage of the bravado brought on by the alcohol to make a suggestion I'd never normally make. "I think Miranda was on the right track. I want to keep things casual this week."

"Like casual sex." Duncan's words come out gruff, and my thighs clench.

"Right. We'll go on dates and we can kiss and..."

"And..."

His hot gaze holds mine, and I nearly jump out of my chair and kiss him.

"And, if we want to," I say slowly, "We'll pick up where we left off six years ago." *In bed.*

"Let's take things slowly and see where they lead." His intense eyes assess me before he says in a careful tone, "But I'll be fucking honest—I've missed you, Brooklyn O'Shea."

CHAPTER FIVE

I smile at him. "You have?"

His cheeks flush an adorable shade of pink. "I have. I don't think I realized how much until you charged back into my life earlier today."

"I've missed you, too." Feeling like if I say more I'll give my entire hand away, I dig my teeth into my bottom lip and go silent.

I haven't slept with a guy in ages. Not for any big reason other than that I haven't found anyone worth taking the time for. Duncan was a hard act to follow, and the few guys I dated in college never got me going the way he had. Once I graduated, I threw myself into my work. When I need to make myself feel good, I've got a drawer full of toys. Toys don't hug me or hold me in the middle of the night when I'm lonely, but they do make me feel good for a few minutes.

Until tonight, I didn't realize how lonely I was for a warm body.

The server arrives with our meal then, and we spend the next little while eating and making small talk.

When we finish our meal, I stand up and make a beeline

for the door. I'm sober now, thanks to all the food, and the reality of what I suggested to Duncan earlier is hitting me.

"How are you related to the O'Shea brothers?" Duncan asks as we exit the café.

"My dad and their dad were brothers, along with Ronen and Shane's father. My dad died when I was two so I never knew him. But while she was around, my mom spent a lot of time with his family, so I did too. And my grandparents continued the tradition, which I'm so thankful for. We all would have dinner together and hang out on weekends. I spent the most time with Killian, Ryder, and Emmett. They were like big brothers to me."

"I'm sorry about your dad."

"Thank you. I'm Brooklyn O'Shea on my birth certificate, but my mom's maiden name is Carter. When my grandparents had to raise me, they thought it would be easier for me in school if I shared the same name as them. They were my mom's parents, so I went by Brooklyn Carter. When I went to college, I returned to my legal last name."

"So you're Brooklyn Carter O'Shea."

"Precisely." I laugh. "You and I both have two surnames. Something we have in common." I raise my eyebrows. "So will you talk to me in Italian?"

"Sei bello."

"What's that mean?"

"You're beautiful."

"That's cheesy."

"Hey, it's true."

"I appreciate you saying that."

He catches my wrist as we reach the corner. "Can I walk you home?"

We both laugh.

"Since it's so out of your way," I tease him. "Actually, I told

Killian I was going to sleep over at Miranda's tonight, so he's not expecting me."

I widen my eyes as I realize how that just sounded, and Duncan's dimples flash.

He puts his arm around me as we wait for the Walk sign to cross the street. "Let's enjoy our walk, and we'll figure things out when we get there."

"Okay."

————

Duncan

The walk home flies by. Before I know it, Brooklyn and I are standing outside my apartment building, the same building where O'Shea's Bar sits on the ground floor. You can't enter the apartments from inside the bar, so we walk around to the back of the building and over to a separate door.

I unlock the secured door and lead Brooklyn up the stairs to the second story where the door to my apartment is down the hall from the O'Shea brothers' place.

Brooklyn glances at me. "We don't know what the hell we're doing, Duncan. And because of that, I think telling my cousins about our plan is a bad idea. Especially since we're going to stay casual. They'll completely flip at that idea."

I don't care what anyone thinks or doesn't think about who I'm seeing, but I get her point. I want to get to know Brooklyn all over again at our pace, and not with her family asking all sorts of questions. I'm not excited about her suggestion to keep things light, but I'm not about to push her.

If casual is all Brooklyn wants, then I'll take what I can get. I've missed her too much to let this opportunity slip. And if I'm really truthful with myself, maybe casual is the best place for us to start. It's what I've done for years, and maybe it's all I'm good at anymore.

I tip my head down the hallway. "Let's go to my place and talk."

———

My plans to talk are upended when Brooklyn's arms wrap around me the second I shut my apartment door behind us.

I spin us around so my arms bracket her against my closed door. "Brooklyn. Wait…"

Any weak effort I had to slow us down disappears when her soft, lush lips land on my mouth. I inhale the taste of honey and sweetness and…her.

"Fuck." I nibble her bottom lip and tangle both hands in her long, blond hair. "I've missed you."

"So kiss me." She tips her chin so our eyes lock. Hers are swimming with emotion.

She looks exactly how I feel. Vulnerable, nostalgic, and yearning for what we had.

"We lost each other too soon," I whisper. "Walking away from you was the hardest thing I ever had to do."

"You deserved to follow your dream," she says simply. "And I was still a kid. I had goals of my own I needed to pursue."

"I know. We always said we'd go big, remember?" I ask her.

She smiles. "I do." She reaches inside the neckline of her shirt.

My heart comes up into my throat when she pulls out a chain with a gold ring attached.

I reach out and touch the ring with my index finger. "Is that…"

"Yours. The one you gave me when we broke up." She

chokes up. "It inspired me. When I felt alone, this ring was my touchstone. But it also made me miss you."

"I wanted to find you a hundred times over the years," I say. "But I promised you a clean break. Anything else would have..."

"Been too hard. I agree. And the thing is, letting me go so I could figure life out on my own was the best thing you could have done for me, Duncan. It hurt when we said goodbye, but even then I knew it was what we each needed."

"We're both grown up now." I reach for the hem of her shirt and lift it until I can drag my hand across the lacy cups of her bra. "And I want you more than ever."

My mouth crashes over hers.

She kisses me back hungrily, and I run my tongue over the seam of her lips, begging for entry. She grants it immediately, and our tongues tangle together.

My mouth shifts from her lips to her neck. I drag my tongue across her heated skin until she moans.

Her body's exactly like I remembered it. But it's different too. Brooklyn's no longer a teenager. She's curvier in all the right places, and I can't get enough of her.

"Sei bello," I whisper in her ear.

"Oh, God." She reaches for the zipper on my pants.

And then, everything happens fast. Too fast, probably.

First, her shirt comes off. Then, my clothes.

Within minutes, I have her naked and squirming in my arms.

I lower my head and put my mouth between her legs.

Holy Christ. She tastes like flowers and Heaven rolled into one perfect concoction.

"Brooklyn, I've missed you spread open for me like this," I murmur into her wet heat. "I want to get you off so bad."

"You will," she vows. "Believe me, Duncan..."

She's starting to pant now.

"You so will..." she says in halting tones. "Oh my God..."

I suck on her clit as I enter her channel with my finger. She's tight and hot and I'm nearly about to come myself.

She moans out my name, louder with each lick of my tongue.

And then she unleashes.

Her legs lock around my head and she bucks against my tongue for so long I'm wondering if she came more than once.

Eventually, her climax slows, and I look up at her. "Was that good?"

She breaks into laughter. "Good? I'd call it fucking amazing. I came twice."

I kiss her bare stomach. "About to be three times."

"Shit, Duncan. You're spoiling me already."

She's still breathing heavily as I struggle to reach my wallet where I tossed it on the table by the bed.

I grab a condom out of it and Brooklyn helps me roll it on.

"Are you sure?" I lean back so I can look straight into her eyes.

"Positive."

She rocks into me, and I slide inside her without another thought.

"Holy..." I bury my face in her neck. "You feel so good. So damn good."

Brooklyn's hips writhe against me. "Oh my God, Duncan. More."

I give her what she wants.

More.

Faster.

Harder.

More. God, Duncan, more.

"Fuck." I lean my forehead against hers. "I'm so close, babe. I'm too close. Let's slow down..."

But Brooklyn cries out. "I'm...coming..."

I feel her clench tightly with my hard-as-nails cock inside her. The sensation drives me over the edge.

"Christ, Brooklyn..." I drive into her as I come harder than I have in years.

The orgasm hits me like a train going full tilt, and it's a long thirty seconds before I can speak or move. When I manage to raise my head, I meet her lust-filled gaze.

"We have to do that again," she says with a husky laugh.

I couldn't agree more.

CHAPTER SIX

Brooklyn

The rest of the night goes by in a sexual blur of kissing, touching, and orgasms. Lots of orgasms. I ride Duncan hard, and then he drives into me from behind, and finally, he bends me over the side of the bed and we come together. Eventually, we fall into an exhausted sleep around four a.m.

The sound of an alarm wakes me.

But when I try to get up, Duncan's strong arm pulls me back against his bare chest. "Don't leave yet," he murmurs sleepily. "We're not done."

My sore body would probably argue him, but I'm still more than willing.

"What time is it?" I glance at the clock on his bedside table. "Shit, don't you have to be at the restaurant soon?"

He leans over me to look at the time. "Crap. I do need to get going. I have a meeting to discuss the bakery opening next door to Bucca's."

I run my palm over his day-old scruff. "You're sexy in the morning. Among other times of day."

He rolls on top of me and kisses my neck. "You're a goddess at any time, Brooklyn. Including now."

Ding!

"The fuck?" Duncan mutters.

"Is that your doorbell?" I'm already scooting out from underneath him and hiding my naked self below the covers. "Is it one of my cousins? I bet it's Ryder. Or Killian. He loves to get up early and go for a run. Does he stop by often unannounced?"

"Hey." Duncan kisses my head. "You're panicking. Don't panic."

"I'm not panicking." *I am so panicking.* "I'm just...curious who's at the door. Maybe you should go find out."

A smile ghosts Duncan's lips. "Okay. I'll go satisfy your curiosity."

"Thank you. And report back!" I say as he throws on his trackpants and leaves the bedroom, closing the door behind him.

———

"It's my sister, Paris, Paris's best friend, Cali, and Cali's sister," Duncan says a few minutes later when he returns to the bedroom. "They want to talk to me about desserts for the wedding. Paris and Caleb have decided to forego a long engagement and get married in a casual ceremony at Bucca's next month."

"Oh, that's so exciting!" I forget for a moment that Caleb is friends with my cousins. "I'll just hide in here until they leave."

"I don't want you to have to hide." Duncan sits down on the bed and cups my chin with his strong hand.

"I just don't want anyone but me to tell my cousins," I say. "They'll definitely need to hear it from me."

"I'll ask them not to say anything." Duncan kisses my forehead. "Don't worry. All three women are trustworthy."

I have no clothes to change into, so showering seems pointless. I throw my jeans and shirt from last night back on and follow Duncan out of the bedroom.

Still clad in only low-riding track pants, Duncan grabs a t-shirt and is still pulling it on as he strides down the hall and into the living room, which is open to the kitchen.

Two dark-haired women and a tall, willowy blonde are sitting on the couch. They all turn as we enter the room. If I'm not mistaken, shock crosses the face of at least two of the women, the two dark-haired ones. The blonde smiles at me like none of this should be any big deal.

"This is my friend, Brooklyn O'Shea," Duncan says. "Brooklyn, meet my sister, Paris, and her best friend, Cali," Duncan gestures to the smiley dark-haired woman and the curvy brunette, both of whom are wearing jeans and long-sleeved fitted shirts. "And this is Cali's younger sister, Carolina," he says as he nods to the blonde. "She just transferred to college in Boston. She's about to turn the big twenty-one," he adds with a smile.

Cali is beautiful and she carries herself with a confidence I wish I had. And Carolina is drop-dead gorgeous. There's no other way to put it. With her skinny jeans, crop top and ballet flats, I'm about to ask her if she models when Paris stands up from the couch and, before I can even speak, she wraps her arms around me in a hug.

"Caleb said he met the O'Shea's little cousin yesterday," she says with great enthusiasm. "It's great to meet you, Brooklyn."

"You too," I say with a smile. "Congratulations on your upcoming wedding."

"Thank you. Will you be in town next month? If so, you must come. You can be Duncan's date!"

I fidget. "Um...that's so nice of you, but I'm not sure..."

"If Brooklyn is free, I'll be sure to take her with me," Duncan says quickly.

"Wonderful. And we wouldn't have come by today if we'd known we were interrupting anything." Paris sends a meaningful look to Duncan. "My brother doesn't usually let women stay the night."

"Paris," Duncan says in a warning tone.

Cali shakes her head and smiles at me. "Don't mind Paris. She's a little too curious for her own good."

Seemingly unfazed, Paris flashes a mischievous smile. "When Cali started to date her husband, London, I was super nosy. I own that part of myself. So." She turns to me and Duncan. "How are you two this morning?"

"Leave it alone, Paris," Duncan says with a frown.

I cross my arms over my chest. "I know I just met you all, and you have no reason to be loyal to me, but I'd love a favor."

"We have reason to be loyal to Duncan," Paris says, her brown eyes warm and kind. "And you seem like a nice person. We're not going to tell your cousins. Don't worry. I've worked at O'Shea's Bar on and off for years, so I know how protective those boys can be."

I exhale in relief. "Thank you so much. I understand how this may look, but..."

"It looks like you two hit it off." Carolina shrugs, her blue eyes shifting from Duncan to me. "What's wrong with that?"

"My cousins are like these three big alpha males who don't think anyone is good enough for me," I explain.

"Got it," Carolina says. "My sister is the same." She winks at Cali, who rolls her eyes with a laugh.

"It's true, though," Cali says. "Us older kids worry about you younger ones."

"I can't believe I never met you before, Brooklyn," Paris

says. "With all the years I've been working at O'Shea's, we should have bumped into one another."

"I'm surprised too," I say. "Although I've only come back to Boston once a year and haven't stayed for long. My job in Manhattan is crazy hours."

Carolina tilts her head as she glances at Duncan and then me. "I find it hard to believe you two never dated before, to be honest. You give off a..." She gestures with her hand. "A couply vibe. I'm a photographer, so I'm always looking below the surface."

"Couply?" I say in a sharp tone. "We're not a couple. We used to...um..."

"Date," Duncan says firmly. "Brooklyn and I used to date. The O'Shea's never knew, and I didn't even know them at the time."

"We met in Paris, France," I say with a smile.

Paris laughs in delight. "That sounds amazing. Tell us more. We all love a good story."

Duncan shakes his head. "Brooklyn can share that sometime if she wants. Right now, let's focus on what you came here for. I'm going to be ridiculously late for my meeting if we don't hurry."

"Okay." Paris opens up her iPad. "Let me show you the dessert options and you can see if they're feasible. We have no time for a big fancy cake, and that's fine by me and Caleb. We just want the wedding reception to feel homey and fun. But with great food."

"Do you bake?" I ask Duncan in surprise.

"He's an amazing baker," Paris says, and I smile at the pride in her voice. "I think he should run the Bucca's Bakery that's opening next door to the restaurant."

I watch Duncan's face as he removes any trace of reaction from it. And I can't get a vibe on how he's feeling.

It's disconcerting. Until I realize why.

He's afraid of losing another dream.

Maybe Duncan and I aren't so different. After all our promises, we actually aren't "going big" after all.

CHAPTER SEVEN

A short while later, Paris, Cali, and Carolina have left, and Duncan is racing to get to work on time.

But I don't want to let this moment pass, not before he heads off to his meeting.

"Hey." I put my arm around Duncan's waist as we stand in his bedroom.

He's dressed and is fixing his gorgeous hair into place. Inky-black with natural body that seems to style without needing product. He really was born beautiful.

"Hey." He stops looking in the mirror and turns to me with a sexy smile. "Do you want me to call in sick?"

I laugh. "Yes but no. Actually, I wanted to ask you about the bakery. Do you want to run it?"

He hesitates. "I'm not sure," he finally says. "Maybe. Maybe not."

"I get it," I say. "Going big can be scary."

He flicks his gaze away from me. "That's not what this is about."

"No?"

"No. Soccer was going big. This is just...a backup plan, I

guess. Even though I didn't know it was there until I had to leave my soccer dreams behind."

"Sometimes life throws us a curveball," I say. "And it sucks. But that doesn't mean your philosophy to go big has to die. You're still that same man, Duncan. Someone who can kick a ball seventy yards when the average person can't kick it thirty-five."

"More like sixty and twenty," he says in an amused tone.

"Fine, so I still don't freaking understand soccer." I hug him. "But you get my point."

"I do. Thank you." He kisses my head.

———

After Duncan and I say goodbye, I hurry down the hall to my cousins' apartment. I use the private entrance to open the door and slip inside the guest room.

I can hear Killian talking in the kitchen. He's clearly on his phone because he says, "Where'd you disappear to last night, Duncan? Ryder and Emmett said they lost track of you at the bar."

I'm safely inside my room with the door shut when I hear: "Brooklyn? You there?"

I pull off my jeans and shirt, grab my bathrobe and throw it on. Tying it around my waist, I open the door a crack. "I'm here. But I'm not decent."

"Will you be home tonight?"

I start to say yes, and then I curse.

"What's wrong?" Killian says from the other side of the door.

"I have a charity event to attend. My boss asked me if I would while I'm in Boston. It's a national organization that raises funds for underprivileged kids, and our company is one of the sponsors."

"That's cool. Are you going alone?"

"Yes, but Miranda and Stella will be there."

Miranda and Stella co-own a Boston coffee shop called Coffee Grounds, and they're providing free coffee for the event.

"Stop downstairs and I'll take you to lunch at Bucca's," Killian says. "I may be able to help you out."

I have no idea what he means by help, but I'll take any excuse to see Duncan again. "Sure. See you then."

———

After taking a long, hot shower, I climb into bed and fall asleep. When I wake up, it's after eleven a.m. I change into a red and white long-sleeved top and white pants before stepping into my favorite pair of ankle boots. I pull my hair up into a high pony as I stare at my reflection in the bathroom mirror.

Last night feels surreal.

I can't believe I kissed Duncan first. I've never been one to wait on what I want—if I like a guy, I see no difference in who makes the first move.

But in this case, I feel like I'm already in way over my head.

I have no clue even how I feel. I know I like Duncan. I know I've missed him like crazy. Anything deeper than that and I shut down.

It's too soon to know. That's normal.

The idea of ending things with him in a week already stings. But I set the rules for a reason. And I really feel a clear ending is for the best.

And for now, I'll enjoy what we have.

I smile as I remember him spinning me around last night and tugging my hair as he drove into me.

The sex was out of this world good. Even better than when we were younger, which I didn't think could be possible.

"Whew!" I blow out a breath and fan myself as I leave the bathroom.

I grab my purse and hail a cab to take me to the North End address Killian texted me.

I notice the restaurant by its sign. Understated but in bright red lettering, Bucca's Ristorante is as authentic as its name implies—I can smell Parmesan and tomato the moment I walk in the door.

And suddenly, I'm starving.

I don't see Duncan when I first reach the hostess stand. But Killian calls out to me from a table, and I head over to him.

I sit down across from him. He's dressed casually as usual in a t-shirt and track pants. "Did you just work out?" I ask him. "You're all sweaty."

He chuckles. "That's because I jogged here. Good way to get my workout in for the day."

"You look more bulked up than when I last saw you. Are you lifting weights?"

"Some. Ryder got me competing with him at the gym."

"You two competing? I'm so surprised," I say teasingly.

"Hey, Brooklyn."

I whip around.

Duncan's standing just behind me. He's wearing a Bucca's shirt and black pants that fit him to perfection. I blink away my lust and keep my expression impassive.

"How are you, Duncan? Killian invited me to lunch."

"That's great."

Killian's phone rings. "I'll take this outside," he says as he stands up and exits the restaurant.

Which leaves Duncan and me alone together.

"I'm glad you're here," he says. "I was going to invite you to come for dinner. Would you like a tour of the kitchen? You can meet my father."

"Of course."

I stand up and as we walk together, he says in a low tone only I can hear, "You look gorgeous."

"Thank you." I glance over at him, and the heat in his eyes sends me into a fit of giggles.

"What's so funny?" an older man asks as we enter the kitchen.

Duncan winks at me before he turns to the man. "Dad, I want you to meet an old friend of mine. Brooklyn O'Shea, this is Roberto Sorelli, my father."

Roberto is a charmer. He kisses my cheek and tells me how beautiful I am.

"And you're smart," he says when I compliment him on his restaurant sign outside. "We worked hard to get that sign just right."

"I'm sure it attracts a lot of customers," I say. "It got my attention from the taxi. I've been working for an advertising firm, and in my professional opinion, you nailed it."

"Really?" Roberto beams. "That's good to hear."

Diego waves from where he's working at the stove, and I call out a hello.

"Let me show you around the kitchen," Roberto says.

As Roberto talks and tells story after story of how he started the restaurant from scratch and plans to pass it down to his nephew and children, Duncan and I catch eyes. A lot.

Diego's the only one in position to see us eye-fucking each other, and he chuckles.

"You're laughing to yourself," Roberto says to him. "Are you losing it, nepote?"

I tense.

"I'm just punchy," Diego says.

"Hello, Roberto," Killian says as he joins us in the kitchen. "Everything working okay?"

"Absolutely," Roberto says as he gives Killian a hug.

I look between them. "You two know each other?"

Killian nods. "We've done handyman jobs at Bucca's for years."

"How come you've never been here before?" Roberto asks me.

"Brooklyn went to school in the suburbs," Killian explains. "She only lived with us for a short while before leaving for college."

"I hope you will come to Bucca's often. We will give you all the food you would like," Roberto says to me with a bow.

"Thank you so much," I tell him.

Killian turns to me. "Before I forget—do you remember Rick O'Brien?"

"No. Who is he?"

"He's in insurance. We went to school together. He's a good guy."

"Okay. That's...nice." *Where is he going with this?*

"I called him on my way here this morning. He said he can take you to your event tonight."

What?!

Duncan chokes on the sip of water he just took. Roberto claps him on the back, and Diego raises his eyebrows at me.

"You need a date, Brooklyn?" Diego asks me.

"No!" I say. "Killian, I never said I needed a date. This is a work thing for me."

"I know. But you said you'd be going alone. I thought you might enjoy the company. Rick will look out for you."

"Good Lord, Kil. I'm a grown woman. I don't need a freaking babysitter."

My cousin holds up his hands in a surrender gesture.

"I'll take Brooklyn tonight," Duncan says abruptly.

All eyes turn to him. He just shrugs. "No big deal."

Killian stares at him. "Are you serious? You think I would trust you to look out for her? We all know your rep."

Duncan's eyes narrow. "You've made your lack of trust clear already, O'Shea. I'm offering to escort Brooklyn to a public event. That's it."

"Good Lord, Kil." I shake my head at him. "You're being rude to Duncan in front of his father."

Killian straightens up and faces Roberto. "I meant no disrespect, sir. I'm just looking out for my baby cousin."

Roberto's eyes twinkle as he glances at me before he turns to Killian. "Your cousin clearly has a good head on her shoulders." Roberto pats him on the back. "I wouldn't worry too much. Duncan is a good boy who obviously cares about Brooklyn."

Killian obviously trusts Roberto because he swivels to look at Duncan. "You're just going to look out for her?"

"I always do," Duncan says, his handsome face expressionless. "I'm sure it will be more comfortable for Brooklyn to go with me than some guy she's never met and probably has nothing in common with."

His tone is gruff, and I'm probably the only one who sees the jealousy flash through his beautiful gray-blue eyes.

I could kiss him for jumping in.

I don't. But I sure as hell plan to later.

CHAPTER EIGHT

Duncan

"Have you thought about what we discussed in our meeting earlier?" Diego asks me later when we're alone in Bucca's kitchen.

"I haven't had time," I hedge as I keep kneading the bread.

"I don't really see what there is to think about, though," he continues while he chops garlic at a mile a minute . "You're fucking good at baking. You're also damn good with customers and with the bottom line. Plus, my uncle and I both think you're the best person to run Bucca's Bakery when it opens later this year. So why are you pushing us off?"

"I'm not fucking pushing you off," I snap. "I'm just not sure I can make that kind of commitment."

"Because then you may end up getting screwed like you did with soccer?" Diego presses.

God, I hate when he does this. But he's completely on target as usual.

I take a deep breath and turn to face him. He puts down his knife and looks back at me. I exhale.

"You're right," I finally say. "But I need a little time to think."

"No problem. As long as you realize why you're delaying. So...subject change—things seem good between you and Brooklyn."

Brooklyn's long gone, but I haven't stopped thinking about her once.

And I certainly don't plan for some insurance guy to escort her fucking anywhere.

"Not your business," I say firmly.

Diego smiles. "I've never seen you like this before. Honestly, I didn't think I ever would."

"Like what?" I say as I finish cleaning up from lunch.

"Protective. Like the only person that matters is Brooklyn."

"She is the only person that matters."

"I get it." He rinses out the heavy pot and begins to prepare for the next crowd of customers. "I'm happy for you. Just don't blow it."

I don't plan to.

But sometimes I worry that my past may blow up my future.

As if on cue...

"Hey, cutie."

I glance toward the kitchen door, where a dark-haired woman is standing.

Maggie something. We went out once weeks ago, but I wasn't feeling it and I said goodbye to her at her door. She's been after me ever since.

And I admit, part of me has enjoyed the attention.

Until Brooklyn re-entered my life. Now, I don't want to talk to any woman but her.

"Good luck with this," Diego mutters under his breath.

"What are you doing tonight?" the woman asks me.

"I've got a date," I tell her right away.

She smiles. "You sure do. I'll do anything you want. I could even cook for you."

I walk over to her. "I'm sorry if I gave you the wrong impression. I'm dating somebody now, and I won't be available again."

She blinks. "Oh. Wow. I didn't think you'd ever commit to anybody. Well, call me when you two break up."

If things work out the way I want them to, Brooklyn and I will never break up.

Maggie bangs the door shut as she leaves, and Diego fist bumps me.

"She'll spread the news," he assures me. "It will get easier."

"It better because Brooklyn doesn't deserve to have to run into my past," I say.

"Killian told me last night that he worries about her in New York City," Diego says.

I jerk my gaze over to him. "He said that?"

"Yeah. He said he doesn't think she ever really fit in there."

I don't know that she did either.

I exhale. "I don't think Manhattan is what Brooklyn needs."

"What does she need?"

A fresh start.

————

I knot my tie and pull on my suit jacket. As I walk down the hall from my apartment to the O'Shea place, I can't believe my good fortune.

"Wow," I say when Brooklyn opens the door.

Her red dress is sleeveless and cut to the knee in an asymmetrical cut. The soft fabric fits her body perfectly, and her blond hair is worn loose around her shoulders.

"You're beautiful," I tell her.

"Thank you. And you're very handsome." She reaches out and tugs at my tie. "The grey color matches your eyes."

I glance past her. "Anyone home?"

She shakes her head as she eases the door shut behind her and loops her arm through mine. "They're already working downstairs. It's just you and me for the night. Except for Miranda and Stella, who I'm sure will be dying to know what's going on. I've avoided talking to them today, so they don't know I spent the night with you."

I escort her to the passenger side of my SUV and open the door. "Knowing the twins, I'm sure they're very curious."

"I didn't know you kept a vehicle in the city," she says. "Do you drive it often?"

"Not for work. But it's good to have, and I have a good long-term parking garage I use."

"You look happy," she says as I step into the driver's side and start the car.

"I am. I get to go on a date with you in public, and Killian gave his approval."

She laughs. "We should definitely thank your dad for that. I don't think Kil felt like he had much of a choice."

I glance over at her as we pull out of the parking lot and head for the highway. "No doubt. But I'm not complaining."

"God, is it wrong to admit that I kind of like sneaking around with you?" Brooklyn makes a cute face as she sticks out her tongue. "I sound like a teenager, don't I?"

I take her hand in mine. "Let's be teenagers together for a little longer."

"You're okay...with being casual?" Brooklyn's voice sounds uncertain to me, but I can't tell if I'm misreading.

So, I give her what I think she needs. "I'm okay with casual," I assure her.

And right now, I am. Because what we're doing feels far from casual. It's real and honest and intense. If Brooklyn wants to label it casual, that's okay with me.

———

We get caught behind an accident on the short drive, and end up hurrying through the hotel where the charity event is being held. When we reach the ballroom, we run into Miranda and Stella by the hot drinks table.

"You two are late," Miranda says with a suspicious glance at me. "Did you stop to make out?"

Brooklyn's cheeks turn an adorable shade of red. "Shh. No, we did not."

Miranda scans Brooklyn's face. "Why are you blushing then?"

"Because I'm here for work and you're talking about sex." Brooklyn glares at Miranda until Stella pokes her sister in the arm.

"Let's wait until afterward to grill her," she says with an apologetic smile at me.

I chuckle. "Miranda, you were the same way when I met you in Europe. I'm glad to see you haven't changed."

Miranda mumbles an apology just as a woman dressed in a formal black gown rushes us.

"Brooklyn Carter O'Shea, you're here!" She looks at me with a wide smile. "And you've brought your boyfriend as well."

"Hello, Linda. Duncan Sorelli is an old friend," Brooklyn says smoothly. "Linda is a work colleague. She interviewed me for this job."

"Brooklyn and I grew up in neighboring towns. Such a small world." She beams at me. "So happy to have you here."

"Thank you. Happy to be here."

"Duncan!" I turn at the familiar voice.

Carolina is walking toward us. "What are you doing here?" she says as she reaches me. "London and Flynn are here representing Shaw, so I tagged along to see if I could help in any way." She holds up her camera.

Brooklyn turns to join us. "I love your dress!" Carolina says to her enthusiastically.

"You're so sweet. You look gorgeous, of course." She touches Carolina's silver dress that drapes loosely over her shoulders and stops just above the knee.

"You do look very nice," I tell her.

Carolina beams. "I got this in Manhattan off the rack for a huge discount!"

While she and Brooklyn keep chatting, I nod at Flynn and London as they approach. The Shaw brothers are well-known in Boston, and the entire room is watching them as they reach us.

Two brothers who look so alike with their dark hair and eyes, they're both dressed in dark suits to match. Both are CEOs of Shaw Integral, a billion-dollar corporation that includes a bank and investment company. Both have been exposed to money and notoriety their whole lives, and yet somehow they've remained down to earth and loyal to the people they grew up with.

London is a painter and more of a rebel with his longer hair, but Flynn is definitely all-go when it comes to running their late-father's company.

I introduce them to Brooklyn, and they each shake her hand.

"How do you like living in Manhattan?" London asks her.

She shrugs. "It's a constant race. That part's hard."

Her eyes go flat, and I realize how tired she looks.

"I used to live there too," London says. "I thought I'd miss parts of the city, but honestly, I really don't."

"I do," Carolina says in a sad voice. "I miss all of New York City."

"You'll get used to Boston soon enough," London says encouragingly.

"Did you just move here?" Brooklyn asks her.

"Not by choice," Carolina says with a glare at London. "I had to transfer colleges. My brother-in-law thinks I'll grow to love it here. I disagree."

Flynn shifts so he can take Carolina's hand. "Let's go get some dessert."

She smiles up at him. "Will you do me a favor and bring me back a cupcake?"

Flynn pretends to grumble, but I've seen the two of them do this dance often. He adores her, and not the way a person adores family.

CHAPTER NINE

Brooklyn

The charity function goes by quickly. Linda introduces me to a number of people in the room including a few coworkers who are in the Boston office. Getting to spend a little time chatting with them helps assuage my nerves about my upcoming transfer. Until Linda greets someone who looks so much like Duncan I do a double-take.

"Starr Sorelli?" I stare at Duncan's twin sister as I see her in person for the first time.

"Do I know you?" she asks in a disinterested tone.

Her fire-engine red painted fingernails graze my palm as we briefly shake hands, and her black hair is piled high on top of her head. She's wearing a slinky royal blue dress that leaves nothing to the imagination.

"I'm friends with your brother."

She shoots me a second look. "You must mean my half-brother, Diego. My real brother has no women friends."

I suck in a breath. "I mean Duncan. We knew each other years ago and just got reacquainted."

"Oh. I see. So you're trying to date him. Well, good luck with that. Duncan doesn't date. Not seriously."

Good Lord, Duncan's sister is rude. So the opposite of Duncan.

"You and Duncan are quite different from each other," I say.

Linda excuses herself to go talk to someone else, and I'm left standing awkwardly with Starr.

"How do you know Linda?" I ask her for lack of anything else neutral to say.

"She goes to my gym. I showed her how to use the elliptical, and she invited me to this event tonight. She thinks I should work in charity."

"Do you want to?"

Starr's grey-blue eyes startle like I've surprised her. "Does it matter?" she says with a shrug. "I need to work somewhere. That's what my father tells me."

"Maybe you could work at Bucca's," I suggest.

"I tried that. It was a disaster. Ask my brother for the details." She looks over my shoulder. "There's Duncan. And what a surprise...he's surrounded by women."

I whirl around. Sure enough, Duncan is in the middle of three women, all of whom are clearly flirting with him. My heart plummets, but I try to keep my expression blank. He doesn't appear to be flirting back, and he steps away from them, but they follow.

All the way to Starr and me.

"Hey." He puts his arm around me. "I see you've met my sister. Don't listen to a word she says."

"Ha, ha," Starr says.

"I'm serious," Duncan says back.

The women drift away as Starr gives me a closer look. Then she looks at Duncan.

"Well, this is new," she says to him with a quirk of an eyebrow.

"Starr," he says in a warning tone.

Before she can respond, Carolina, with cupcake in hand, shows up and asks if she can help me with anything.

"Sure," I tell her. "Let's go find Linda and see what you can do."

As we walk away, Carolina whispers, "Starr was terrible to my sister when they first met. Don't let her get to you."

"I won't." *I totally did.* And seeing Duncan surrounded by willing women didn't help.

I put all of that unpleasantness out of my mind as we walk through the large room. "So Flynn got you a cupcake, huh?" I ask.

Carolina laughs. "He and I like to screw with each other. He gets me back all the time, trust me."

"You two seem to have some...how do I put it? Insanely hot chemistry."

Carolina stops short and stares at me. "Is it obvious?"

I nod. "As the sun on a hot summer's day. Has no one ever mentioned it before?"

"No, not really." She drops her voice. "Flynn is completely off-limits to me."

"How come?"

"My sister and his brother. They would flip. They think Flynn is too old for me, and that I'm fragile."

"You seem perfectly capable," I say, and I mean it.

Carolina loops her free arm through mine and we start walking again. "That's why I like you. You're probably the only person in Boston who thinks that."

I want to ask her more, but we bump into Linda, who's thrilled to have another set of hands.

Carolina sticks closely to my side throughout, and I get

the sense she's even lonelier than I am. She turns out to be incredibly useful as well; Linda utilizes her photography skills to take pictures all night.

"We can definitely use some publicity for this event," Linda says to me. "My boss said not to invite the press, but he's certainly not going to turn down free photos. We'll put them all over our social media."

Duncan finds me a few minutes later.

"Are you okay?" he asks me.

"I'm fine." I glance behind him, where a redhead is staring at Duncan like he's a snack she wants to eat.

He takes my hand in his. "Are you sure?"

"Yes." I smile at him, but it feels forced.

"Let's go to the buffet and get some food. You must be hungry."

For the rest of the evening, Duncan and I manage to have a great time.

We're about to say our goodbyes when Linda beckons me aside.

"I keep meaning to ask if you're related to Antonia Carter," she says.

Only my tight grip on my glass of champagne prevents it from shattering to the floor.

"How did you know..." I ask, flustered.

"We lived in neighboring towns, remember? There weren't any other Carter families but your grandparents."

"Right." I swallow and try to make sure my voice sounds even. "Of course."

"I considered not saying anything, but I so loved your grandmother," she says quietly. "We were in the theater together."

"Oh," I manage to say politely. "How nice."

"What a shame," she says, her gaze filled with that

emotion I always see when someone brings up my family to me.

Pity.

"And when your grandfather died next..."

"Yes," I say in a clinical tone. "They were wonderful people and I miss them."

"Of course." Linda pats my arm. "It broke my heart to hear of their granddaughter being left all alone. Now that I know you and see how wonderful you turned out, I'm relieved. But if you ever want to talk..."

No, I don't want to talk to someone I hardly know about a brutal piece of my past.

I reach for my polite face when I say, "Thank you." I down the rest of my champagne in one gulp. "It was nice seeing you."

Forcing the moment out of my head, I turn around and walk back to Duncan.

I feel myself shutting down the way I always do when my family is mentioned. The kind of shutting down I'm not good at coming back from quickly.

"You okay?" Duncan asks me quietly. "You've gone pale."

"I'm fine," I lie.

"You're not," he says, dipping his head so we're at eye level. "Talk to me."

I read the worry in his gaze.

"I can't," I say. "Not here."

"Later then," he says. "Let's get out of here."

"Please."

Duncan makes good on his word. Before I know it, we're out the door.

London, Flynn, and Carolina go home, but Starr asks us to go out for a drink. Duncan glances at me and starts to decline the invitation, but the twins say yes and beg me to come with them.

Miranda and Stella took a taxi, so Duncan drives them and Starr too. Miranda's joking about some guy who hit on her at the event, and she gets me laughing like she always does. I feel myself relaxing again, and I do my best to forget my awkward conversation with Linda. That moment is exactly why I didn't want to move back home.

CHAPTER TEN

As we reach O'Shea's, Killian waves from the bar, and before I can stop her, Miranda invites him to join us. He says he'll stop by our booth in a few minutes when he gets a break.

Starr disappears somewhere in the bar while Killian gets us all drinks. Duncan stays behind to chat with Ryder while Miranda, Stella, and I head for our booth. As I look back, a tall blonde is leaning close to Duncan. I stop walking and watch as he turns away from her. But she keeps trying...until Duncan physically steps backward and makes it beyond obvious that he's done talking.

Is this how it always is with him? He walks into a room and women can't stay away?

I slide into the booth across from Miranda and Stella, who's smiling slyly at her sister.

"So. Miranda, are you and Killian..." Stella starts to say.

"We're nothing." Miranda frowns. "I just figured why not say hi."

Stella and I glance at each other and go silent.

"What about you and Duncan?" Miranda asks me. "Fill us in."

"I asked him to do casual like you suggested, and he said he was fine with that." I bite down on my lip.

"He says he's fine with casual," Miranda repeats.

"Right." I glance away from her and tug at the skirt of my dress. We're all still wearing our dresses from tonight, and I feel out of place in the relaxed atmosphere of the bar.

"I guess I shouldn't be surprised. I was hoping he'd want more than that."

"Miranda, you said to go for casual."

Miranda rolls her eyes. "That's because I'm a firm believer that guys suck. And I thought it may help you. But when I look at your face, I'm not so sure. How do you feel about it, Brooklyn?"

The honest answer would be that I've been replaying my conversation with Duncan over and over in my head.

"You're okay...with being casual?" I asked him.

"I'm okay with casual."

He sounded comfortable with it.

And yet...so much felt unsaid between us.

But I'm determined to handle our imminent break-up better than I did six years ago. So I answer Miranda more calmly than I probably should.

"I plan to use this week to do exactly what you recommended—to let go of my past with Duncan once and for all," I say confidently. "You know, *goodbye past, hello future.* I think the whole thing will prove to be extremely healthy for me."

Stella raises her eyebrows.

"Okay, fine, it's borderline stupid," I say in frustration. "But I'm tired of pining away for a guy I lost my virginity to in high school. I have to take Duncan down off the pedestal I've had him on in my memories. He's clearly a player—he's got women flocking to him."

"What happened tonight?" Stella says. "Were women all over him?"

"There were some women," I admit. "He didn't flirt back."

"But did he know them from the past?" Miranda asks. "Like, did it seem as if they..."

"Had already slept together?" I finish for her as she trails off awkwardly. "I don't know. I saw them flirting with him from a distance."

Like a car wreck you see up ahead.

"That must have stung," Stella says with sympathy in her voice. "You care about him so much, and they probably barely know him. Except maybe what he's like in bed...ow!"

I glance at Miranda. "You don't have to kick her to keep her quiet. I've had the same thoughts."

"Honey, maybe you should end this thing before you get hurt," Miranda says in a gentle tone. "I'm sorry I pushed you. I just wanted you to..."

"Get over him." I take a big sip of my beer. "I know. Me too. And if I can't do it this week, I hate to think what my love life will be like in the future. I haven't been able to date like a normal person because I've compared every single guy to the impossible—a summer from my youth. In Paris no less. It wasn't reality. It was like a romance story that isn't real life. I had Duncan built up so high in my head from the moment I met him."

"I get it. But what if you can't stop the train?" Miranda says. "I'm the world's biggest cynic, but even I can't deny that your chemistry together is off the charts. And Duncan Sorelli is hotter than hot. If you weren't with him, I might even do him for a night."

"Ha." Stella sticks out her tongue at her sister. "You would never have a one-night stand."

Miranda shrugs. "Never say never."

Stella and I look at each other in surprise.

"Well, none of that matters," I say. "Because like I said, Duncan and I didn't have a one-night stand. We agreed to keep seeing one another for a week."

"So what would you call it?" Miranda asks me. "A temporary affair?"

"Sure. That works." *Sort of.* "A temporary affair," I say calmly as I tear at the tiny rip in my napkin until it splits in half.

"Brooklyn, you're destroying that napkin." Stella's eyes widen at the paper carnage developing in front of me.

I continue shredding my napkin. "Surely I can handle a week of being naked with a hot man and having no strings. It's simple, really—lots of sex, which so far has led to lots of orgasms—and then we part politely at the end."

"Part politely?" Stella breaks into a loud laugh. "But you two will both be in Boston."

"Remember, my cousins don't know yet," I remind her.

"But Duncan does?" Miranda asks me.

"I told him, yes."

As Stella glances past me into the bar, she puts her finger to her lips. Two seconds later, Duncan slides into the booth next to me.

CHAPTER ELEVEN

"Killian's about to join us." Duncan runs his hand over my leg underneath the tabletop. "He got a little sidetracked," he chuckles as he gestures behind us.

I look where he's pointing and cringe when I see Killian standing a few feet away with Margaret Mannion. She's wearing a tight O'Shea's Bar t-shirt and a mini skirt. She's hot, and she knows it. She was also not my favorite person growing up.

"Margaret's probably the worst server here," Miranda snaps. "She grew up in our town, so we know her well. She was a shitty student in high school, and from the looks of it, she's still lazy now."

"I don't know about that," I say jokingly. "She looks to be working quite hard—on her mission to nab an O'Shea."

Killian glances up and catches my eye, and I raise my eyebrows at him. He extricates himself from Margaret's arm, which is locked firmly around his torso, and heads to our booth.

He takes a seat next to Miranda, who's still scowling.

"Aren't you busy?" she snaps as Killian puts his arm across the back of the booth.

"What's that supposed to mean?" he says innocently.

"Margaret was trying to score with you," I say.

Killian shakes his head. "She talks a mile a minute. I couldn't get away from her."

"Right," Miranda mutters.

As Killian turns toward Miranda to plead his case, I lean closer to Duncan without planning on it.

He begins to trace invisible lines on the thin material of the dress covering my thigh. I dig into my bottom lip as goosebumps hit my arms. Duncan keeps trailing his fingers softly up and down my leg, and I look up to catch Stella's amused gaze.

I swallow as I edge myself away from Duncan's hand. My hormones are enthusiastic as hell, but my heart is vulnerable, and I need to remember exactly what Duncan and I are doing here.

We're reconnecting.

We're figuring out how to say goodbye properly.

But those two things are the opposite of one another. Which means I need to take a deep breath and calm my pulse.

Duncan Sorelli is wonderful. And yes, he remembers our time together in Paris fondly. I truly believe him when he says he missed me.

But my cousins aren't stupid. When they say Duncan has a reputation in Boston, I know all too well what that means. Duncan is genetically blessed, and he clearly doesn't have to take a step without a female approaching him.

I saw it with my own eyes on our first official night out together, and I need to make sure I remember that when my heart starts wanting more than just a week of good sex.

Because Duncan may be amazing in the bedroom, but a monogamous relationship isn't something he seems comfortable with. At least not anymore.

"So, Duncan," Stella says with a glance in my direction. "How do you like Boston?"

"I love it," he says. "It's so much smaller than New York City. I feel at home here."

"New York City can be lonely," I say out loud without meaning to.

"That's why you don't fit in there.," Killian says. "Same as I wouldn't."

"How do you know who would and wouldn't fit in where?" Miranda says. "Brooklyn has lots of interests that are different from yours. So do Stella and I."

"Oh, yeah?" Killian looks at her. "What interests you, Ran?"

Miranda's face turns red.

I furrow my brow as I look toward Stella. Is Miranda...

"Yes," Duncan says in a tone only I can hear.

I flick my gaze to his in surprise. "She's..."

"She's interested in him," he says close to my ear. "It's plain as day."

"I can't believe I never saw it," I say almost to myself.

At the kick to my shin, I raise my eyes to meet Stella's amused ones. "She never wanted you to know," she mouths to me.

Miranda would kill us if she knew we were talking about her, but she's far too distracted by my cousin's presence.

Killian puts his arm around Miranda and murmurs something into her ear. Her cheeks turn even redder and she mumbles what looks like, "Fuck off."

Duncan takes off his suit jacket and loosens his tie. "I'm glad I don't work in corporate," he mutters.

I reach for my phone in my purse.

You look hot in suits.

His phone dings and he fishes it out of his pants pocket.

He grins, and I watch as he fiddles with the keys.

I've put my phone on silent, so Killian's never the wiser when Duncan's text pops up on my screen.

What about in a t-shirt and jeans?

Hmmm. You're right...still hot.

"Did you two have fun at the function tonight?" Killian asks, his gaze sliding from Duncan to me.

I pat Duncan's shoulder playfully. "He was the perfect date. And I also would have been fine there on my own. Either way, you didn't have to worry, Kil."

Duncan's warm hand lands on my thigh again and he adds, "Your baby cousin is an adult now. Maybe it's time to cut the leash."

Killian's blue eyes soften. "Maybe so. I still think of her as a kid."

"Like me and Stella?" Miranda's eyes behind her glasses are cold as a winter's night when she turns to Killian. "You've known us for years and you act like we're still teenagers. We're all grown-ass women, you know."

He clears his throat as their gazes lock. "I know." Then he abruptly says his break is over and he leaves the booth.

I reach for my glass and swallow down the last of my beer. The conversation turns lighter as a buzzed Stella starts peppering Duncan about soccer and whether or not the players wear cups.

As the evening wears on, I'm wondering how the heck I can surreptitiously leave with Duncan. But it turns out I don't need to worry, because when Killian pops by our booth, I learn he's otherwise preoccupied.

"I've been thinking," he says to Miranda. "You and Stella should stay over at our place tonight. It's safer."

Miranda grumbles, but I don't miss the interested flash in her eyes.

"You can share the guest room with me," I say, already plotting the evening out in my mind.

CHAPTER TWELVE

A half hour later, Stella's climbing into bed in my guestroom, and Miranda and Killian are still downstairs.

"Go now," Stella urges as I take off my dress and throw on jeans and a sweatshirt. "The guys will never know you're not here."

"I hate lying to them," I say. "But you know what they're like."

"Over-the-top nosy in their little cousin's business." She nods. "I know quite well. You and Duncan deserve to figure out your shit on your own, Brooklyn. Don't feel guilty—this white lie isn't hurting anyone."

Maybe not, but lies, however well-intentioned, don't tend to stay under wraps forever. The thing is, I have something I need to do tonight. And Duncan is the only person I want with me when I do it.

I hug Stella goodbye and slip out of the apartment.

Duncan lets me in the second I knock.

I take his hand. "Grab your keys. I want to leave before they close up downstairs."

———

Duncan

I have no idea where we're going, but Brooklyn tells me to head north, so I pull onto the highway.

Something knocked her off at the end of the charity event. I don't know what it was, but she was shaking when we left the hotel.

She seemed to recover her energy at the bar, but when I glance over at her in the passenger seat, she doesn't look back at me.

"You okay?" I say. "You seem lost in your own thoughts."

"It makes sense for us," she says in a quiet tone, almost like she's talking to herself. "You and I met during a turbulent time in my life, and then we broke up. We never got closure," she says abruptly. "I guess that's why fate put us back in the same city."

My chest constricts. "So we can have closure?"

She squeezes my hand. "You were such a comfort to me that summer, Duncan. You were my strength when I had none of my own. But now, I'm okay. So saying goodbye this time shouldn't hurt as much."

I lace her fingers through mine and let out a rough breath. "Babe, saying goodbye isn't like a math equation. You can't make it easy just because you know what's coming next."

"Maybe so," she says softly. "But I can prepare myself better this time."

I want to ask her why she's so insistent on planning our demise, but I keep silent. For some reason, Brooklyn's guardrails are steel right now. And asking her to take them down won't work. I have to show her I'm worth going the distance for.

———

Brooklyn

I lead Duncan through the dark parking lot and up to the locked door of the old converted barn that's now a community theater in the small town outside Boston.

"Brooklyn, where are we?"

I pull a key out of my purse, a key Grandma gave to me before she died. I've never used it, never thought I would come back here. But Linda got me all sorts of emotional, and here I am taking a walk down memory lane.

I flick my gaze over to Duncan. "I'll explain in a minute."

I thought coming here would help me. I thought being buzzed would make it easier. But as I stand outside the theater, I can barely stop my hand from shaking as I unlock the door and push it open.

I pause before stepping inside.

"My grandmother used to perform in this theater."

Duncan kisses my forehead lightly. "Have you been back here since she passed away?"

I shake my head. "No. I couldn't..." I cut off. "I'll explain more inside."

The hallway is dark, but Duncan finds the light switch easily, and we walk together down the short corridor, past the closed ticket window, and into the lone room in the place.

The stage is dark, but the curtains have been left open.

I stare up at the stage as the memories hit me.

Grandma acted her heart out in this theater.

"She loved performing," I say almost to myself. "She came alive here."

Duncan takes a seat on the edge of the stage and I hop up next to him. He puts his arm around my shoulders as he scans the room.

Rows of empty seats stare back at us.

"What are you not telling me, Brooklyn?" His voice is quiet.

I take a deep breath. "This is the place where my mom dropped me off for the last time. Before she took off for parts unknown."

The words come out more bitter than I'd expected.

"I don't hate her anymore," I say. "I really don't. But she left me with her own parents because she didn't want to play the role anymore."

That's what I truly believe my mother thought she was doing—playing mother rather than actually being one. She thought she could stop doing it when she grew tired, and she did.

Luckily for me, her parents were responsible adults. They took us in and raised us themselves.

Duncan's arm tightens around me, and I lean my head on his shoulder.

"Have you ever heard from her?" he asks me.

"Once. She came back to town and stopped by the house. I was fourteen." I sit up straight and pick a piece of lint off my jeans. "She didn't know me at all. We sat awkwardly in the living room while Grandma made tea for all of us and Grandpa tried to keep talking about anything he could think of. At one point, he rambled on about the lawn mower for over five minutes, and all Mom and I could do was stare at each other. We exchanged numbers, and after tea, she left. I tried her once, but her number was disconnected. I haven't heard from her since."

"Shit." Duncan pulls me into his arms. "I'm sorry, Brooklyn."

I laugh awkwardly and jump off the stage. "This is a real downer of a date, huh? I never would have come here tonight except..." I trail off.

"Except what?" His gray-blue eyes assess me. "What happened at the charity event? I know something's been bugging you."

I focus past him to the stage, where I can still see Grandma smiling broadly for her curtain call. She was so loving and nurturing, and I still find it hard to reconcile that with her daughter. Maybe mothering skills skip a generation sometimes.

"Nothing much," I say. "Linda told me she knew Grandma from the theater. Something about our brief conversation triggered the memory of my mom walking away from me. It sounds stupid."

"It doesn't." Duncan catches my wrist and tugs me until I'm standing between his legs dangling off the stage. "And you're not anything like your mother, honey."

"I didn't say..." I stumble.

"You didn't have to." Duncan tucks his thumb under my chin so I can't look away. "I know that's what you're thinking. You'll be a great mother—if that's something you want to be someday."

I've never allowed myself to think about being a mother. It was a role I didn't think I could ever play. But I want to let go of the moment when my own mother walked out of my life.

"Thanks for coming with me tonight," I say to Duncan.

He searches my face. "You know I'll go anywhere with you, Brooklyn."

The air thickens around us as Duncan continues to look at me.

"You certainly have a lot of women interested in you."

The statement is out of place in this stark moment of pain, but I've never been good at keeping my thoughts to myself.

He swallows. "I'm sorry about my past. I wish to God I hadn't lost myself in meaningless nights of..."

"Of what?"

"Of numbing." He wraps his arm around my back. "I

always feel when I'm with you. And when we said goodbye to each other, I never felt close to anyone like that again."

"Me neither. I just didn't hook up with loads of men. I used toys instead."

He gives a bare smile. "That's too erotic of an image for this heavy conversation, Brooklyn."

"Sorry," I say with a wink.

I break the moment by stepping back and spinning around in a circle. "So. What do you think of the small-town theater vibe?"

"It's awesome. I didn't know your grandma, but from what you've told me, I can imagine her being right at home on the stage."

"She would have liked you."

I bite my lip. The pull of what's always between us overwhelms me, and I step forward and kiss him.

As his lips move hungrily over mine, the sadness I always have when I step into this theater is immediately muted.

Duncan's arms go around me, and I climb onto his lap.

"Nobody's here," I whisper into his ear.

Duncan responds by nibbling my neck until I shiver.

His hand moves down my back and slowly down to my ass, all the while kissing my neck.

But then he hesitates.

"Brooklyn," he says in a raspy voice. "Maybe we should wait. I know this place has a lot of emotion for you, and not all of it's positive."

He's right. Being here for the first time in years is harder than I'd expected. But I want to look forward, not back.

Wrapping my arms around his neck, I lean in and kiss him again.

CHAPTER THIRTEEN

I only mean for it to be a quick kiss before asking him if he's ready to go.

But every kiss with Duncan always feels so right. I never want to rush my time with him.

I also never want to stop. Our quick peck turns into a long kiss, and Duncan tangles his fingers in my hair and pulls me close to him.

We break away with both of us breathing heavily. Our eyes lock and hold.

"Brooklyn. You're so damn sexy..." Duncan takes my face in both his hands and slants his mouth over mine again.

Something about this whole evening feels like Duncan and I are crossing a line we can't come back from—some sort of agreement to take this one-week affair seriously.

But I'm far too gone with lust for him to overthink anything right now.

A noise escapes my throat, and my lips part as Duncan's hot tongue enters my mouth.

Oh, God. The way he tangles his tongue with mine should

be illegal. I let my head fall back and shift my body closer to his.

When I feel his erection pressing into my stomach, I moan into his mouth.

"Are you sure this is okay?" Duncan says in a husky voice.

"I'm sure. Keep kissing me," I say.

He licks my lower lip before nipping it with his teeth, then he circles every inch of my mouth with his tongue.

In my effort to get even closer to him, we lose our balance. Duncan shifts until he's on his back, taking me with him.

And any walls I had come tumbling down.

I don't know where this is going. I don't know what the hell we're doing. The whole thing is surreal.

But one thing is clear—I want Duncan more than ever.

We roll across the wooden stage as we continue making out.

When we roll into the curtain at the back of the stage, we both start laughing.

"We got a little out of control," I say.

Duncan brushes my hair out of my face and helps me up. "I like getting out of control with you."

I straighten my shirt, which had ridden up my torso. "Maybe we should go somewhere private."

"Sounds good to me." He takes my hand. "Are you sure you're ready to leave?"

I squeeze his hand. "I'm sure."

———

We don't see anyone when we return to Duncan's apartment.

He leads me down the hall to his bedroom, and we shut the door behind us.

Duncan turns on his bedside lamp, giving the room a soft

glow of light. He sits on the edge of the bed and pats the spot next to him.

"Do you want to talk?"

I shake my head. "Not right now."

I reach for the bottom of my shirt. As I pull it over my head, Duncan's breath hitches sharply.

I toss my shirt to the floor and step in between his legs. He lifts me up until I straddle him.

His lips touch mine, and I rock into him, needing to feel his hardness against my core. "I want you," I whisper.

He unhooks my bra, and the straps slide off my shoulders. Without taking a second to delay, he immediately takes my aroused nipple in his mouth. The sensation goes straight to the ache between my legs.

"Oh God." I run my hands through his hair and pull him tighter against my breast.

Duncan sucks, licks, and nibbles at my nipple. He uses his hand to stroke and caress my other breast until I cry out. He rolls us back onto the bed and unzips my jeans just enough that he can slip his hand inside.

When he reaches the lace band of my panties, he groans and runs his thumb along the underside until I'm delirious with need.

"Duncan..." I grip his wrist with my hand. "Touch me."

"Getting there," he promises.

Slowly, his fingers slide underneath the band of my underwear.

As soon as his rough pads reach my wetness, he stills. He rests his forehead against mine, and his eyes search mine.

"God, Brooklyn." His gray-blue eyes are so close to me I could count the sparkling silver flecks if I tried. "Being with you again is..."

"I know." I plant kisses across his mouth and cheeks. "It's intense."

Duncan pulls his hand out of my panties slowly. "We were so wild last night. And it was incredible. But tonight, I want to take our time."

He pulls his shirt over his head in one motion, and soon his bare, muscled chest is against mine. We roll and Duncan pulls me on top of him. I kiss my way from his lips to his neck and then over his hard chest and abs. He groans loudly, and I love that I can turn him on like this. Making out with Duncan is something I've fantasized about since we parted years ago, and I reach for the zipper on his pants.

I slip my hand inside his boxers, and we both cry out at the same time.

He kicks his pants and boxers off of him.

"You're beautiful," I tell him honestly.

He looks down at me through his dark lashes. "Yeah?"

I laugh. "Seriously? You're unsure of yourself?"

"With you," he says and I look at him in surprise. "With you, Brooklyn, I'm unsure."

I take a deep breath. "Duncan," I say softly. "You're gorgeous. You have the most beautiful body I've ever seen. But more importantly, you're beautiful on the inside, too."

He flashes a teasing smile. "So you think I'm hot?"

In response, I lean down and kiss the tip of his hard length. He groans as I put my mouth around him. I watch him from underneath my lashes as he threads his fingers through my hair.

"Brooklyn," he mutters. "You don't have to do this..."

Moving excruciatingly slowly with my tongue, I surprise him by abruptly taking as much of him inside my mouth as I can.

"Holy..." Duncan's voice comes out hoarse as I suck hard on him.

"Brooklyn, I'm not going to last if you keep going." He

gently pulls my head away from him and flips us so he's on top of me.

He peels my jeans and underwear off, never taking his eyes from mine. His hands move down to the curve of my ass, and he uses the leverage to pull me tightly against his naked body.

"I want to make love to you in so many different positions I don't know where to start," he whispers into my ear.

"We did a lot of positions last night," I smile.

"However you want to, as slow as you want to, I'm good with anything."

Before I can answer, he reaches between my legs and massages my throbbing ache in torturous circles.

"Oh God," I slam my eyes shut. "Duncan, don't stop."

"You're so damn wet."

I feel a finger slide inside me slowly, and then his mouth is on me. And for the next minute, everything is complete bliss.

Within seconds, I go over the edge. I call out his name as I come down from my high, and when I open my eyes, I see him putting on a condom.

He pushes inside me easily and braces his arms on either side of my head as his mouth lands on mine.

"Every time is better than the last," he mutters as he kisses me hard.

I know.

And with each time we're together, I fall for him even more.

Duncan and I fit. I've only dated a few guys, but none comes close to what this feels like—Duncan buried inside me, and I'm so turned on I'm already close to coming for a second time.

I wrap my arms around his muscled back as he begins slowly moving in and out of me.

The ache inside me just grows more intense, and my hips

buck underneath him. Wrapping my legs around his waist, I rock with his thrusts, wanting all of him inside of me.

"Harder?" he asks, his eyes on mine.

"Yes," I beg him. "Harder."

His mouth crashes down urgently on mine again, and we start moving together desperately like our bodies have missed each other too much to be patient. I feel my climax building strong and fast, and just as Duncan calls out that he's close, I start coming.

"I'm right there," he says as he follows me into orgasm. "Fuck, Brooklyn..." He holds me close to him as we both come down from our highs.

"Sex was never our problem," I say with a smile as Duncan holds me close.

"No. Still isn't." He kisses my cheek. "Timing was our only issue, honey. Maybe this time..."

He trails off like he doesn't want to scare me.

And I appreciate that. He's being thoughtful, especially after what I told him tonight about my mom. I've been clear that we should look at this as a one-week affair.

So I'm surprised at myself when I echo his words back to him. "Maybe this time."

CHAPTER FOURTEEN

"Baby girl, I'm leaving."

"Where are you going, Mommy?"

"Far away. You won't see me for a while."

"Take me with you!"

"I can't. You stay here with Grandma. She'll take care of you while I'm away."

She spins and starts walking away. She walks so fast I can't keep up with her.

"Don't go! Please!"

"Brooklyn. Babe. Wake up."

I open my eyes.

Duncan is lying next to me. His hand's on my shoulder and his eyes are filled with concern.

"Sorry." I sit up. "Bad dream." I glance at the clock and see that it's nearly dawn.

"Do you still have that nightmare a lot? The one where you lose your grandmother?"

My nightmares these days are about my mom and not the night my grandmother died. But I don't tell Duncan that.

Because that confession will bring up things I've been

trying to suppress. Like this feeling of foreboding I've had since I returned to Boston.

I haven't shared my anxiety with anyone. A bad feeling doesn't always mean anything. I force a smile and pat Duncan's cheek.

"You'll need to get ready for work soon," I say. "I'll go now before any of my cousins wake up."

I've got my shirt on and my underwear by the time Duncan reaches me in the bathroom.

He scoops me up over his shoulder and tosses me gently back onto the bed.

"Talk to me." He cages me in with his arms.

"I can't." I curse a single tear slides down my cheek. "I really can't."

Duncan cups my cheek with his large hand. "I'm your friend, too. Not just your lover. We were friends first, remember?"

I do.

That's partly why us becoming lovers was so amazing, and so easy. I already trusted him.

"Let's hang out after work, okay?" I give him a kiss.

Duncan walks me to the door and kisses me long and slow.

"My cousins are in town tonight," he says. "The hockey players. You remember me mentioning Hunter and his three brothers?"

"Your mom's sister's kids?"

He nods. "Hunter's the one I keep up with. Probably because he's closest to me in age."

"I don't follow sports much. Did they make it to the pros?"

"All four of them," he says, and I can hear the pride in his voice.

"Wow, that's amazing. Are they playing Boston tonight?"

He reaches over to the side table and produces two tickets. "Come with me. It will be fun."

I hug him. "I'd love to."

———

I bounce up and down in my seat at the arena. The place is packed for the New Orleans Fire versus Boston Fighters game. "I've never been to a hockey game before!"

Duncan's eyes brighten. "I love seeing you excited."

"You'll have to explain the game to me," I say. "You know I've never been a big sports fan."

"You learned a lot about soccer when we were in France."

"That's because I wanted to learn a lot about you." I bump his shoulder with mine. "You were my main course. Soccer was just a side dish."

He smirks. "I like what you did there—bringing food into the conversation."

"Right? It's like merging your current life of the restaurant with your past."

He turns serious. "That's a good analogy, Ms. Carter O'Shea."

I flush with heat and try to switch topics. "So your mom and Hunter's mom were close?"

"They were. My aunt passed away, but she was a really nice person."

"Did their dad raise all four boys by himself?"

Duncan hesitates. "He did, but he...died also."

His tone sounds strange, and I don't push for more of the obviously tragic backstory.

"How terribly sad," I murmur as the game starts.

I'm immediately transfixed by how fast the game moves. The puck is everywhere and I honestly have trouble following where the heck it is half the time. Duncan points out his two cousins—Hunter and Liam Storm—on the New Orleans team.

And gosh, I may know next to nothing about hockey, but those boys are intense on the ice. Especially Hunter. He scores two goals and assists on a third as New Orleans wins the game handily.

When we meet him and Liam afterward outside the lockers so we can take them for a drink at O'Shea's Bar, I learn that both Storm brothers are good guys.

Hunter and Liam both greet Duncan with big hugs.

"Sorry we can't come eat at the restaurant," Hunter says genuinely. "We'd love to see your dad and eat some amazing Italian food."

Duncan introduces me next. Both brothers greet me warmly. They've got dark, wavy hair and piercing green eyes. Not to mention bodies that look like they belong to pro athletes. And did I mention their Southern accents? Duncan told me Liam is married but that Hunter is single. I can't imagine he will be for long.

"Your accents are so charming," I say to them.

"Thank you, darlin'," Liam says.

I giggle.

Duncan steps even closer to me and puts his around me possessively. "Tesoro," he says.

"What?" all three of us say.

"Italian," he says casually.

Liam breaks into a laugh. "Oh, so that's how it is, huh?"

Hunter winks at me. "My cousin's not too subtle."

I smile to myself. Duncan's definitely showing his competitive side.

After we leave the arena, we drive to O'Shea's. Shane, Ronen's older brother and a big hockey fan, comes over to say hello. Shane and I are cousins too, but he and Ronen lived in

Maine for years, so I don't know them well. I'd recognize the dark hair and handsome Irish looks anywhere though.

Shane ushers us over to the circle of couches behind the bar so no one can bother Hunter and Liam for photos or autographs.

"If anyone bothers you," he says, his expression serious. "You let me know. I work as a bouncer here when they're short-staffed. I'll make sure no one messes with you."

Taking a look at Shane's tough exterior and hard body, I don't doubt he would.

After he's left to fill our drink order, Hunter looks between Duncan and me.

"So how long have you two been dating?"

Killian stops by right then with our drinks.

"No, we're not like that," I say quickly to Hunter.

He shoots me a surprised look.

"It's a rather long story that I can share later. Or Duncan can," I ramble.

Killian, a fan of all sports, is too busy being a fanboy over the two hockey studs to pay any attention to what I'm babbling about.

"Your team has got to be favorite to win it all this year," he says to the two guys. "Boston sucks right now, so I'm pulling for you."

"Thanks, man," Liam says. "Appreciate the support."

Miranda and Stella show up then, and the group of us have a fun time hanging out. Stella and I ask Hunter and Liam lots of questions about New Orleans, and Miranda keeps everyone entertained by her flirting slash eye rolls at Killian.

Liam and Hunter have to leave to catch the team plane, and Stella decides it's much easier if she and Miranda can just stay with me again.

Which makes it all the easier for me to slip into Duncan's apartment.

"This is getting to be a habit," I joke as I snuggle into his bed later that night.

Naked and warm with Duncan's arms wrapped around me, I feel safe and happy.

"So what does that Italian word mean that you used earlier?"

"Tesoro?"

"That's the one."

"Darling."

I laugh. "You don't have to worry about competing with your cousin. I only have eyes for you."

"That's good because I feel the same. We have another soccer game tomorrow."

"Yay!" I groan. "That means my cousins will be there. I enjoy being with you so much more when they're not around."

He strokes my hair. "Did you want to talk to me about your bad dream?"

I tense. "It was about my mom. It's just a bad flashback, really, of when she left. I don't have the nightmare often, but it always throws me off. I don't know, sometimes I think I got stuck in that moment when she walked away and my whole life has been kind of controlled by my reaction to her decision. Does that make sense?"

"Yes. But..." He whispers in my ear, "Sei piu coraggioso di quanto credi."

"Okay, that gave me shivers because it sounds so romantic and sexy." I turn in his arms to face him. "But what the hell does it mean?"

"You are braver than you think." He kisses my cheek, and I nearly melt.

"Thank you." I kiss him lightly on the lips. "You always know what I need. Like the game tonight."

"I had fun," he says.

"I did too."

"Brooklyn..." He pauses.

"What is it?" I look up at him.

"This feels right. And not just because we knew each other before. You feel right now—as the woman you are today."

"I think I'm falling for you," I say in a bare whisper.

"You're not the only one falling." His voice is rough and needy. "And I know you don't want to talk about anything past this week, so we won't. But I am enjoying the hell out of this week, Brooklyn."

My walls come down a little bit more. Okay, a lot more.

Duncan shifts so he can kiss me soft and slow.

And then our kiss turns to hard and urgent. Just one of the many things I love about being with Duncan.

Nothing is ever boring or the same. It's always-changing and always passionate.

As we drift off to sleep after another long lovemaking session that ends in yet another incredible orgasm, I touch my fingers to my lips.

Things are getting intense between us.

And right now, I'm feeling the ache in my chest for when we'll say goodbye.

I've said goodbye so much in my life.

It should be easy for me.

And sometimes, it is.

But with Duncan, saying goodbye always sucks.

CHAPTER FIFTEEN

"Hey."

I had snuck into my cousins' guest room just before dawn, and Miranda and Stella were asleep.

I spin around in my bed. "Did I wake you?"

Miranda's staring at me from her sleeping bag on the floor. "When did you get here?"

"Not too long ago." I raise my eyebrows. "What about you? Did you and my cousin..."

"No," she snaps. "We just talked. Argued, is more like it. Killian's an ass."

"He can be," I agree. "But he certainly seems interested in you."

"He's not. He thinks of me like a little sister."

I smile. "Didn't look that way to me."

"Or me." Stella's head pops up from next to her sister. "He's into you, Miranda. I'm sure of it."

At the knock on our door, I call out, "Yeah?"

"We've got soccer practice tonight so Shane's running the bar. Do you ladies want to meet us at the field and we'll get dinner after?" Killian calls out.

I glance over at Miranda, who scowls.

But Stella quickly calls out, "Sure, sounds good! We'll meet you guys later."

Miranda and I both glare at Stella.

"I don't enjoy hanging out with my cousins and Duncan at the same time right now," I say. "It stresses me out."

"I didn't say yes to stress you out," Stella says. "I said yes for Miranda." She puts her arm around her twin. "I think you and Killian would make a cute couple. But you're both so stubborn. So you need to hang together more."

"Whatever." Miranda flushes pink and then turns toward me. "I'm sensing that you're considering telling them about you and Duncan."

"If Duncan and I just hook up for the week, then no. If we..." I trail off.

"Get serious?" Stella fills in.

"Right. If we do that, of course I'll tell them. But tonight isn't the time for confessions. Duncan and I are still getting to know each other again."

CHAPTER SIXTEEN

Duncan

"Ready?" Diego calls out from the middle of the field.

"Ready." With the soccer balls at my feet, I pause motionless and wait.

When Killian calls out, "Go!" I kick the first ball at the moving pylon with the target at the top.

"That's one!"

I'm already at the second ball. I let it go, and it hits the moving pylon again, right on the white target painted at the top.

"Two!"

Soccer ball number three leaves my foot.

When it slaps against the pylon, directly on the target paint, Caleb, Diego, and Killian start clapping and cheering.

Ryder and Ronen give me high-fives.

"Impressive, man," says Flynn, who is joining Team Bucca's this month.

"You would have been a huge star," Ryder says admiringly.

Normally, that comment, while well-meaning, would sting and linger for a while afterward. Tonight, though, it washes over me without much bite. Maybe Brooklyn was right—it can be possible to go big in more than one thing. If your first dream doesn't work out, try again.

"Maybe." I shrug. "I like my life now. So it's all good."

I glance over at the sideline.

And I suck in my breath.

Brooklyn just arrived with Miranda and Stella.

She might as well have come alone for all I notice the other two women.

Brooklyn's hair is tied up in a messy ponytail; she's wearing a button-down pink shirt that's untucked over black jeans. She's stunningly beautiful, and when she smiles at me and waves, I have to restrain myself from walking over and taking her in my arms.

Knowing we have an audience and Brooklyn wants to keep things private, I stay where I am and smile back at her. Emmett, Ryder, and Killian are off to the side having a kicking contest and they aren't paying attention.

But somebody is.

"Who are you grinning at?" Caleb turns to look. Then, he whips back to me. "Shit, Duncan. You're still flirting with the O'Shea's little cousin?"

I stare him down. "Keep it down. You want them to hear you?"

Diego claps me on the back. "Caleb's not going to talk. But if you don't want them to suspect anything, you might want to stop eye-fucking Brooklyn in public. Save your flirting for later."

Caleb glances over to the sideline again. "So you two are dating?"

I open my mouth and then close it. I don't know what the hell we are. To label it feels silly, anyway.

"They clearly go back," Ronen says simply. "I understand how that is."

I look at him gratefully. He and his girlfriend, Ava, have a long history, and they finally became a couple this summer.

Caleb crosses his arms over his chest. "I think you two look great together, but don't fuck with her."

"It's none of your damn business," I mutter.

"I'm getting married in a couple weeks, and I assume you'll be bringing her." Caleb slaps my back. "You're certainly welcome to. But I don't want any drama between you and the O'Shea's. Paris deserves a perfect day, which makes the guest list my business."

"I'm not fucking with her, you asshole." I grab the soccer ball out of his hand. "Practice isn't over yet. Let's go."

Brooklyn

"Duncan sure can kick a beautiful pass," I say, my eyes fixed on him as he arcs a soccer ball downfield to Diego.

"Sports are so boring," Miranda complains, her focus fully on Killian as he lifts the bottom of his shirt to wipe sweat off his brow.

Stella and I laugh. "You look real bored right now," I tease her.

"Well, I am." She turns on her heel and heads for the wooden bench a few feet away. "Isn't their practice over yet? I'm ready to go eat."

"They're show-offs," Stella says in amusement as Killian tackles Diego by the goal just as Duncan arcs a perfect strike to Caleb, who taps the ball into the net. "Especially Duncan. He looks like he's a professional surrounded by novices. But all of them are having fun. They may never leave."

"Kind of like how the three of us could hang out and chat all day," I say. "Speaking of, let's go sit with Miranda while the guys go shower and change. Maybe we can get her into a more relaxed mood before we go to dinner."

———

Despite the awkwardness of being with my cousins and Duncan at the same table, dinner turns out to be fun. Paris and Carolina join us, along with Diego's girlfriend Shohanna and Ronen's girlfriend, Ava. The table is long and manages to fit all of us, and it feels like a big social gathering.

Shohanna also works in finance and she tells me about an opening at Shaw Integral. "I'm leading the interviews for this particular position, and I'd be happy to schedule you for one ahead of time," she says, her blue eyes warm and friendly.

I smile and accept her kind offer. This is something I've missed in Manhattan. I would go out with co-workers weekly for drinks, but I never hit it off with anyone the way I do with Miranda and Stella.

And having family nearby is more of a relief than I want to admit. My cousins are nosy and bossy, but they love me, and I'm enjoying being around them again.

I leave for the bathroom, and when I step out of the restroom, Duncan is leaning against the wall. He gives me a kiss, and I laugh and tell him he needs to wait until we're alone.

"We are alone," he says as he gives me another kiss. "I don't see anybody around."

"Wait until we're in your bed," I whisper into his ear.

I pat his chest and head back toward our table. Duncan is a step behind me when I turn out of the hall and head left. As I get a view of our table, I spot a woman standing next to Ryder. He rises from the table and faces her. Then Killian and Emmett stand too. They move to either side of Ryder like it's a stand-off. What the hell...

The woman's face is obstructed by her hair, but Ryder's is clear as day to me—his blue eyes are blazing with anger, and his mouth is set sternly like he's about to tell this person off. Ryder doesn't show his anger often, so when he does, it's a big deal.

I can't hear what he's saying until Duncan and I get closer.

"...what do you want?"

"I heard you've done very well with your dad's bar," the woman is saying. "I'm so proud of you, honey."

"Don't call me that," Ryder says with feeling.

I pull up next to him. "What's going on?" I ask him.

Killian looks over my head to Duncan standing beside me. "Will you take Brooklyn home?"

"Sure."

I look up at Killian. "Why do I have to leave?"

When he doesn't answer me, I turn to look at the woman.

She has blond hair that's cut in a blunt chin-length style. She's wearing a lot of mascara and heavy foundation, but it can't hide two things. One—she's older than she's trying to appear. And two—*her light hazel eyes are the exact same color and shape as mine*.

Something twists in my chest.

No.

It can't be...

I clutch Duncan's arm, suddenly feeling my legs weakening.

"Who are you?" I hear myself say to her.

"*Marie*." Ryder's tone is so sharp I jump.

Marie.

That was...

"Mom?" I stare at the woman, who's staring back at me. "You're my mother?"

"She's not anyone's mother," Ryder says in that same sharp voice. "She doesn't deserve that title."

"Yes, Brooklyn." Marie—Mom—says to me. "I'm your mama." She reaches out and gives me a hug. "I've missed you. You're all grown up."

I stand still as a statue while she hugs me. Inside, I'm shaking, but I don't show that on the outside. When she pulls back, I cross my arms over my chest.

"What are you doing here after all these years?" I ask.

"I wanted to see you and your cousins," she says, averting her gaze.

"She wants money," Ryder says in a lethal tone. He pulls out his phone and punches something into it before looking back up. "Her husband divorced her because she was cheating on him. He left her with nothing, and she's got piles of debt. She's looking for an easy fix to her problem. What else is new?"

I stare at this woman who was supposed to be there for me. The woman I've missed having in my life so much that it hurt.

"You're here for *money?*" I say in disbelief. "That's what it took for you to come back here and look me in the face? Or did you not even know I'd be here and you just came to harass my cousins?"

"Honey." Marie steps closer to me. "I'm your mother. I'll always love you."

She reaches out to touch my shoulder, and I wrench back, nearly stepping on Duncan's foot. "Don't touch me," I spit out.

CHAPTER SEVENTEEN

Duncan

This is starting to spiral. Ronen's gotten involved in the conversation now. He stands up and tells Marie she needs to leave the restaurant or he'll ask security to remove her.

I don't think security's going to get a chance with the O'Shea's about ready to haul her out of here themselves.

I put my arm around Brooklyn's shoulders just as Emmett wisely says to Marie, "Let's take this outside. We're causing a scene."

Diego, Flynn, and Caleb start to rise from the booth, but I motion to them to stay with everyone else at the table. Those guys will back us up if we need them to, any place, anywhere, but I don't want Marie to think she can draw even more of a crowd. By the look on her face, she's the kind of person who seeks attention, and the less of us giving her that, the better.

With my arm still around Brooklyn, we follow the O'Shea's as they exit the restaurant with Marie and round the corner to a private alleyway.

"You said that you'd wire me the money," Marie says accusingly to Ryder.

Her eyes are stone cold without a hint of warmth in them. They may be the same color as Brooklyn's eyes, but nothing else is at all similar. Her face is harsh with angular cheekbones and a pointy chin. She looks like she hasn't loved a day in her life. Maybe she used to be softer, but life got in the way. Whatever the reason, she and her daughter couldn't be more different as they stand across from one another.

Brooklyn spins on Ryder. "You've been in touch with her?"

He puts his hands up. "Just for the last month. She came to the bar after her marriage fell apart." He grimaces. "London happened to be there."

Shit. London is one of the wealthiest men in Boston.

"She'd seen his feature in the paper about his painting."

He doesn't say any more, but I can read between the lines. That article mentioned London is the billionaire CEO of Shaw. It also mentioned O'Shea's Bar. London, because he's always looking out for people, was trying to drum up press for the O'Shea's. It apparently unwittingly attracted some leeches also.

"I didn't know our family had such wealthy friends." Marie glances at me. "Who are you? Do you work for Shaw also?"

I don't bother to answer her.

Instead, I turn to Ryder. "Is she blackmailing you?"

He hesitates.

But I know him too well. No way would he be in this position if she wasn't threatening something.

He takes me aside and murmurs, "She has a local tabloid lined up to tell her story. Using my connection to London and Flynn, they're going to say she's related to the O'Shea's by marriage, and she's agreed to talk about Brooklyn and how her parents stole Brooklyn from her. You know how the press will blow it up. London and Flynn are public figures, and I don't want Brooklyn's name dragged into anything."

Neither do I.

I run my hand down my face. "How do you want to handle this?"

His phone dings, and he glances at the screen before answering me. "I've texted our family attorney. He just told us to meet him at his office. We'll settle this now." He turns to Brooklyn. "Duncan can take you home. You and I will talk when I get back."

Brooklyn's already shaking her head. "I'm coming with you. I want to make sure this woman never blackmails you again."

————

When we arrive at the law office, the O'Shea's attorney says she has the paperwork ready. I take a seat in the waiting room while they all head for an adjoining office.

As Ryder, Emmett, and Killian start walking away, Brooklyn glances back at me.

I cock my head at her. "Do you want me in there?"

She turns back and comes to stand in front of me. "It's okay. My cousins will think it's strange."

"I don't care what anyone else thinks right now," I say. "I care about you. And if you want me there..."

I see the second she shuts me out. Her bright eyes go flat and she gives a quick shake of her head.

"No, it's okay," she says firmly. "I'll be fine."

She waves goodbye and turns away. I watch her disappear into the office and shut the door behind her.

Brooklyn's tough as nails. She's been through more than she should have had to go through, and she's come out on the other side.

But everyone has a breaking point.

Seeing her mother for the first time in forever, and having that mother still be so self-absorbed and shallow...it's got to be crushing.

Something shifts inside of me. The vulnerability on her face as she stood in front of me...it twists me up inside.

And I know I need to up my game if I don't want to lose her.

CHAPTER EIGHTEEN

Brooklyn

"You okay?" Ryder asks me for about the fifth time since we parted from our mother.

I break into a fit of laughter, no doubt a completely inappropriate reaction for the moment. But I learned a long time ago it's better to laugh than to cry. And right now, if I don't laugh, I'll probably bawl.

Ryder insisted on the four of us sitting down in their living room for a cup of tea. Duncan went over to his place to give us some privacy, and when Ryder was distracted unlocking the door, Duncan mouthed "I'll be here" as he walked backward to his apartment. For the moment, I'm glad it's just my cousins and me because my emotions are all over the place.

"I'm fine." I clear my throat. "No, I'm not fine. I'm shitty. But I don't want to talk about that right now."

"Okay." Killian reaches for the remote. "Let's watch a movie."

"Look." I turn to all three of my cousins. "I love you. And I know you're trying to help, but the way you protected me today was more than enough. You got Marie to sign the papers saying she'll never talk about any of us to the press or else she'll end up in court. You paid her off with your hard-earned money, and she also had to sign that she'll never ask for anything else from us again and that she'll never come near us. You did everything you could possibly do, and I adore all of you. Thank you."

Emmett's blue eyes flash with anger. "She got off easy. The way she treated her kid is criminal."

I lean my head against the couch cushions. "My Grandma must be rolling over in her grave. She and Grandpa both."

Killian blows out a breath. "Your week back home has certainly been a roller coaster."

"Did she say anything to you when she left?" Ryder asks me, his eyes watching me carefully. "I saw her lean in close to you."

Yes, that's true. We all left the law office together, and when the others turned to say goodbye to the lawyer, my mother whispered to me, "I really did wonder about you over the years."

"Then why didn't you ever check on me?" I asked her, angry at myself for not keeping the hurt out of my voice.

"I came back once," she said. "I parked across the street and watched you playing out in the front yard with your grandmother. You seemed happy. I knew she was doing a better job with you than I could. So I left."

"That's a cowardly decision," I said. "I wondered about my mother every single day. Where were you, and why would she choose a life apart from her child?"

Her eyes, which had looked so empty, sparked with pain. Real pain that she quickly brushed aside by blinking. When I looked again, the pain was gone and her gaze became vacant again.

We parted shortly after that.

And I've been mulling over our exchange ever since.

I tell my cousins what happened.

Ryder frowns. "Don't let her actions affect you, Brooklyn. She didn't know how to be a mother. It was nothing you did."

"I know." Logically, I know that. "Today was just overwhelming. Seeing her out of the blue like that." I glance at him. "Were you going to tell me she'd contacted you?"

"Absolutely. But I wanted to get everything worked out before I involved you."

"I get it. You were trying to protect me just like you always have." I pat his arm. "But you can't think of me as a kid anymore, guys. I'm not made of glass. I won't shatter if things get tough."

"You're the strongest person we know," Killian says. "We just think you've been through enough shit for a lifetime."

We chat for a while longer and then we put on a movie. Like usual, the guys, exhausted from working at the bar around the clock, are asleep within the first hour.

When I go to throw blankets over them, they all half wake and and stumble into their bedrooms.

Alone in the living room, I glance at the clock, wondering if Duncan's already asleep. After what happened with my mother, spending the night by myself to think would probably be best.

But as I sit on my bed and never-ending thoughts of my mother flash through my mind, the last thing I want is to be alone.

———

Duncan

"Is Brooklyn all right?" Diego asks me over the phone as I enter my apartment.

I toss my keys on the coffee table and drop onto the couch. "I hope so."

He stays silent like he's waiting for...

"Fuck," I say in frustration. "I hate that I can't be there for her."

"You *were* there for her," Diego says. "You stood by her side the entire time. But I get what you're saying—you had to conceal that she's yours."

I go quiet.

Brooklyn's mine.

And I want to be hers.

That's exactly right.

"She's pushing me away," I mutter.

"Understandable," Diego says. "She looked shell-shocked. She was white as a sheet."

I know. And I know the sudden re-emergence of her mother—I hate even calling her that when she abandoned Brooklyn and clearly doesn't give a crap about her—has to sting hard.

"I need to talk to her," I say.

"Not yet," Diego cautions me. "She has to talk to her cousins first. I'm sure they have a lot to work out."

He's right. I tell him goodbye and flip on the television. The screen lights up with some action flick I barely pay attention to.

When it ends, I glance at my phone and check the time.

It's late.

She's probably sleeping.

She probably wants to be left alone.

But the pain that crossed her face when she looked at that woman and realized who she was...it gutted me.

And I'm not going to sleep until I know she's okay.

CHAPTER NINETEEN

Brooklyn

I've changed into an oversized t-shirt and yoga pants when my phone dings with a text from Duncan.

How are you doing?

I've been better, I type back.

Do you want company?

I text him back quickly.

Come over. Use the private back entry.

I open the door to the guest bedroom a crack and watch down the hallway.

Within a minute, Duncan's door opens and he steps out. He closes the door behind him and turns to face me.

We stare at each other for a moment before, hands in his jeans pockets, Duncan heads toward where I'm standing in the open doorway.

"Hey." He takes my hand and tugs us both inside.

He shuts the door behind us before taking me in his arms.

"Are you okay?" he whispers. "I'm sorry about all the shit you just had to deal with."

I gaze into his worried gray-blue eyes. Eyes that have seen

me through the worst of times and that are now here with me again for another doozy.

"You always seem to be around when I'm going through something difficult," I say. "Some would call that Fate."

"Some would." He searches my expression. "What would you call it, Brooklyn?"

I sink down onto my bed, and Duncan joins me. I shift to my side so I'm facing him. "I'm not sure what to call it. You're always there for me. I don't think I deserve it, to be honest. I'm used to figuring problems out on my own."

"And you're amazing at it. You and I aren't that different honestly. I learned as a kid that if I wanted to follow my dreams, I had to be my own biggest fan. You know my mom isn't exactly mother of the year material either. I'm not comparing her to yours, of course, but I do understand the yearning for quote-unquote normal parental love."

"I know you do." I touch his cheek. "I'm so happy you were finally able to get that with your dad."

"Me too."

I reach out and gently trace his lip with my finger. "I'm proud of you."

"Hey, how'd we end up talking about me?" He strokes my hair. "You're the one who was just dealt a blow tonight. How are you holding up?"

I tell him about what my mother said to me, and his face darkens.

"I'm sorry," he says. "My words don't matter, but I wish to God she'd been there for you."

I swallow down the lump in my throat. "She left me to her parents, and I'm very grateful for that. It could have been a lot worse. It just sucks that she still doesn't want a relationship with me. I shouldn't be surprised, but I guess I was anyway."

"She doesn't deserve you," Duncan says as he takes me into his arms.

"I want to forget about all of it," I murmur into his shoulder. "Can you help me do that?"

His strong hands are warm on my back. "I can try. What do you want to do? We could go out for coffee or..."

My mouth lands on his. "I don't want coffee," I say into his lips. "I just want you tonight, Duncan."

"You have me, Brooklyn," he says as he flips me onto my back and crawls over me. "Whenever you want me, you have me."

Tomorrow, I'll wake up and remember how my mother walked away from me for the second time in my life. But for the next few hours, Duncan makes good on his promise to help me to forget all the pain of tonight.

CHAPTER TWENTY

Duncan

I take the next day off. And I spend it with Brooklyn. All we do is have fun. We have lunch at Bucca's, drinks at O'Shea's, and we find a way to have our alone time.

Drinks are with Diego, Shohanna, Paris, and Caleb, Miranda, and Stella. Carolina slips into the bar unnoticed by the staff, and Paris invites her to join us at the booth.

"I'm not twenty-one yet, but I do have a fake ID," she says with a wide smile.

Stella laughs. "I remember those days."

"Absolutely not," Diego says firmly to Carolina. "Your sister would flat out kill us all."

Carolina pouts. "Fine. I'll just have water."

"So, are we the only people who know you two are fucking like rabbits?" Miranda asks me and Brooklyn.

Diego chuckles.

"Yes," Brooklyn says to her. "Let's keep it that way, okay?"

Carolina's blue eyes sparkle. "I love an illicit romance. You two should keep it secret for as long as you can."

"Don't encourage her," I say only half-joking.

Brooklyn smiles at me. "I'll go public if you want to."

I turn to her. "Seriously? You're ready?"

She nods. "If you are."

"Babe, I'm definitely ready."

"Not tonight, though," she says. "I need to plan our big reveal."

"You could do one of those gender reveal parties," Carolina suggests. "But it would be a relationship reveal. Inside the balloons would be a photo of the two of you in a compromising position."

At the look on Brooklyn's face, Carolina amends that to say, "Or a romantic photo of you two sharing a kiss or hug."

"I don't think my cousins would have the patience for any kind of balloon-popping reveal," Brooklyn says. "They'd probably just ask what the hell we got balloons for and move on to the food and drinks."

"You could do it at our wedding!" Paris says. "It would be so fun!"

"No way," Brooklyn and I say at the same time.

"I would never upstage you like that," Brooklyn adds.

I tug on Brooklyn's hand. "Let's go figure this out on our own."

Everyone laughs as we leave the booth.

"You're staying with us tonight, remember?" Miranda says with a wink. "You haven't revealed yet, so the secret has to continue."

———

Brooklyn and I walk up Charles and through the Boston Common to the movie theater. We share a bowl of popcorn and a soda and hold hands through the film.

Afterward, we walk along the Charles River and talk.

"Shohanna graciously offered to interview me for an open

position at Shaw," she confides in me. "Whether I get the job
or not, I'm going to tell my cousins I'm moving here. It's
time."

She grins at me, and I smile. Her cheeks are flushed pink,
and her hair is blowing in the ocean breeze. She's beautiful.

"You seem like you're excited about moving," I say.

"I think I am. I'm nervous, but not as nervous as when I
moved to New York City. This time, I'm coming home. Plus,
I have you."

She says the last four words casually, but my chest aches
with need. I stop walking.

"Brooklyn."

She looks up at me with wide eyes.

The moon is nearly full, and it shines brightly off the
water.

And I can't hold back anymore.

"You remember I wanted to say something to you when
you left Paris?" I ask her.

"I asked you not to," she says hoarsely. "I said it would be
too hard to walk away."

"You did." I pause. "Can I say it to you now?"

She sucks in air. The moment is deadly quiet before she
looks me straight in the eyes and whispers, "Tell me."

I take both her hands in mine.

"I love you," I tell her, saying the words for the first time
to someone else. "I love you, Brooklyn Carter O'Shea."

CHAPTER TWENTY-ONE

Brooklyn

"*I love you. I love you, Brooklyn Carter O'Shea.*"

I stare at him. "Duncan..."

"I know you weren't ready to hear it back then." He wraps his arms around me and kisses the top of my head. "And I understood why. You'd just lost the last parental figure you had. You were in no place to give your heart away to me."

"I did, though." I look up at him through my tears. "I did give you my heart, Duncan."

He kisses my lips lightly. "I feel like I just blindsided you."

"You didn't," I say. *You did. In a good way, but still.*

"I did, and I wish I hadn't." He pulls me in close for a hug. "You're dealing with the aftermath of seeing your mother for the first time in years." He leans back to look at me. "I have an idea. I'll walk you home, and we'll spend tonight apart. You deserve to have the space to think about everything. You didn't get that time last night."

"Oh...okay." Deep down, I know he's completely right.

Even though my body wants him. But my body will always want Duncan. Right now, my heart needs some time.

"And just so we're clear," he says as he drops me off at my apartment door. "I want to date you for real, Brooklyn. I want to do what we never did before...make this thing between us permanent. Not fleeting or temporary like it's been in the past. I want to be here for you forever."

"Forever?" I say in a whisper.

"Yes." He kisses me one last time before taking a step back. "I'm not going anywhere. I'm not going to run off. I'm not going to turn my attention elsewhere. I'll be here."

I wave goodbye to him until he disappears inside his apartment.

And then I step into my cousins' guest bedroom and sink onto the bed.

Duncan Sorelli loves me.

No one has told me that since my mom. My grandparents weren't openly affectionate that way. They hugged me all the time, but they didn't say I love you to each other or to me. Which was fine. I knew I was loved. And my cousins adore me. They'd do anything for me. But the O'Shea's are not the most emotionally expressive bunch.

And when Duncan said the words, I realized how nice it is to hear them.

The tears are coming before I've even laid my head on my pillow. Tonight I will feel all the things I've buried. And tomorrow, when I get up, I'll step forward into my future. Duncan and I deserve that. We've waited long enough.

CHAPTER TWENTY-TWO

The next day, Duncan gets called into work for an unplanned busload of tourists. Bucca's is packed for hours. And that night is the second charity soccer game.

Which seems just about perfect for what I want to do.

I call Miranda and Stella, and they pick me up in their red VW bug. We find parking so freaking far away from the game that Miranda complains we might as well have just walked. Which is probably true.

There is a small crowd when we arrive, and the game is about to start. My cousins are milling around on their side of the field by the bench, and Duncan is with Caleb and Diego on Bucca's side. When Duncan walks into the middle of the field to prepare for the start of the game, I know this is my best chance.

"Go now," Miranda urges me.

I run onto the field. Out of the corner of my eye, I see Killian turn and notice me.

"Hey!" he calls out.

I ignore him and keep running toward Duncan. Killian will know why I'm here soon enough.

Duncan's back is to me, but like he can feel me coming, he turns.

He breaks into a grin.

But before he can speak, I launch myself at him. He catches me in his arms as I wrap my legs around his waist.

"Hey, beautiful," he says.

"Hey." I kiss him hard.

I can hear the reaction from the crowd behind me, but I don't care about anyone but the man holding me.

"You're the only man I've ever loved," I tell him as I choke up. "I couldn't tell you in Paris. I was too young and in too much pain. But I did then and I do now—I love you, Duncan Sorelli. I always have."

Duncan's gorgeous grey-blue eyes that have always seen the real me beneath the pain fill with tears. "Ti voglio bene."

"Oh my God, I love when you talk to me in Italian." I look at him. "What did you just say?"

He whispers into my ear, "I love you."

"What the..." Killian, Ryder, and Emmett are walking toward us.

I wave at them as Duncan hugs me tight.

"Let's go big," I whisper to him.

He pulls back and winks at me. "I'm all in, babe."

EPILOGUE

Duncan

"I do," Paris says with tears in her eyes as she looks at Caleb standing across from her.

"I do," he says as he picks her up and kisses her.

Paris giggles, and next to me, Brooklyn wipes a tear off her cheek. "That was a beautiful ceremony," she says.

It was.

As I watch London, Cali, and their toddler daughter, Joy, follow Paris and Caleb down the makeshift aisle at Bucca's, and then Diego and Shohanna, I feel grateful for the woman by my side.

I never thought I'd have what they all have. I was so busy running away from my lost dream that I didn't see what was right in front of my face. I told my dad this morning that I'd love to run Bucca's Bakery.

I'd also love to marry Brooklyn. And the ring in my pocket is practically jumping out on its own.

"Go big" was a little joke Brooklyn and I had between us in France, but underneath the lightheartedness was a truth we each needed to live by: don't let loss and heartbreak define your future. Don't let pain win.

"Hey." Brooklyn turns and kisses me as we head for the tiny dance floor that my dad set up. "You okay?"

"I'm perfect." I kiss her back and then gently shift us so we're alone in the corner of the room. Couples dance by us, laughing and talking. London and Cali, Diego and Shohanna, and Ronen and Ava.

Then there are those whose relationships are undefined, like Flynn dipping Carolina while she nearly tumbles out of his arms because she's laughing so hard. He steadies her and whispers something in her ear that makes her blush.

Starr is in heated conversation with Ryder at the edge of the dance floor about something. I didn't even know my sister knew Ryder that well, and I give them a second glance before they disappear in the crowd.

My dad passes by with his wife, Bianca, and they both give me the thumbs-up behind Brooklyn's back. They're the only people I've told what I plan to do.

When no one is paying us any attention, I kneel down in front of Brooklyn, whose hands go to her mouth. "Duncan, what the hell are you..."

I pull out the ring box and open it. "Brooklyn Carter O'Shea, I love you. Will you marry me?"

She's on the ground with me in an instant. Her arms go around my neck as she kisses me.

"Yes, I'll marry you!"

I don't know the odds, but I know most people don't end up with their first love. Brooklyn and I bet on fate, and we got the biggest gift of all—a second chance.

In order to seal the deal, we had to take a risk. And we did. We went big. And I'm grateful I had the chance.

———

Thank you for reading Boston Player!

Click HERE for Hunter's full-length standalone second chance hockey romance or **turn the page** to read an excerpt.

WHAT'S NEXT

Turns out we both need to score ... A Second Chance Hockey Romance in the Storm Brothers series.

Duncan's cousin, Hunter Storm, gets a new roommate—and she turns out to be an old flame. CHECK OUT **HUNTER**, a full-length standalone and book 1 in the Storm Brothers series, **HERE**! And turn the page to read the first three chapters.

Hunter

I can't be alone. But I can't be in a relationship. And now I can't even score on the ice.

I'm in a slump.

I figure an off-limits pet sitter is just what I need. Until I see who the agency sent me.

Winter Allen is standing all grown up at my front door.

She's my hat-trick: the looks, the heart, and the history.

I let her run off to Broadway because she deserved to follow her teenage dreams as much as I did.

We both got everything we wanted. So why does she look so damn lonely?

Winter

I didn't plan to see Hunter Storm again. And I don't plan to tell him why I'm back home in New Orleans.

But after one devilish grin, my body tells me Hunter's the only man who can help me.

Turns out we both need to score again. So who's to say it's a bad idea to mix his fire and my gasoline?

What are we doing? I'm not sure, but it feels too good to stop.

Turn the page to read the first three chapters of **HUNTER**!

HUNTER

Chapter 1

Hunter

I check the defender hard into the boards and win the battle for the puck.

Spinning around, I cradle the prize with my stick as I skate down the open ice toward the goal.

The goalie pushes out from the net to try to narrow down my angles, but I'm going too fast. With a quick flick of my wrist, I launch the puck off the end of my stick.

It zips past the goalie's outstretched glove but sails wide left and misses the net.

"Fuck," I growl as I race behind the goal.

I slam into the first defender before he reaches my errant shot, and Murph dislodges the puck from between him and the boards. Murph looks up and sees that Liam has a clear path to the net, and he sends the puck toward him. Liam fakes like he's going low with his shot, and at the last second, he flips the puck up past the goalie's stick and into the back of the net.

I breathe out in relief as the buzzer sounds.

"One to nothing," Liam says as he pounds me on the back. "We've still got a shot to win the division."

But when we skate over to the bench and file off the ice, Coach Jones isn't smiling.

"Nice going." Coach slaps Murph and Liam on the shoulders before turning to me. "You do what you need to do to get out of this funk, Storm. You hear me? Whatever it takes. You're our first-line left winger. I want to keep it that way."

His warning isn't subtle, and I know he meant it that way.

"Understood," I tell him. "I'm working through it."

"You need my help, just let me know."

"Yes, sir." I continue past him.

"Whatever it takes, Hunt," Liam says to me as he echoes our family motto. My brother's tone is determined like always. "Right?"

"Right."

Once we're off the ice and out of earshot of any media or coaches, Murph mutters to me, "We need you, Hunt. We got lucky tonight."

Dean, our best defenseman, catches up to us as we head for our lockers. "Fuck, yeah, we did." His blond hair is sweaty and sticking to his head as he removes his helmet and throws it into his locker. "We should have beat those guys going away."

I grimace. This slump has stretched for nearly four weeks. All of January, and now that we've hit February and nothing's changed, I'm starting to panic. But I don't say that.

Prior to January, I'd been having the best season of my career. There was talk of league MVP, and I was stoked. Lately, all that talk has cooled, and I just want to get back to what I know I'm capable of.

It was always my dream to play hockey for my home state of Louisiana—not to mention with my brothers. So when the New Orleans Fire got an expansion team three years ago, and my oldest brother, Liam, and I were picked up, it was a dream come true.

Our twin brothers, Jared and Max, were still under contract for the Montana Wild Kings, but New Orleans was able to snag Camden Murphy out of free agency. Murph is my childhood friend and brother in everything but his last name, and the three of us are feeling pretty damn lucky. We've got a great owner who's all in, and I want to pay him back for bringing me here by playing at an MVP level. But I can't do that unless I get myself out of this damn slump.

I open my locker and toss my helmet onto the shelf. I take off my skates and then start to strip off my jersey and shoulder pads.

"I know what the problem is," a familiar deep, gravelly voice says from my left. "You miss living with me, don't you, baby brother?"

I glance up. Wearing nothing but a towel around his waist, Liam leans against the locker next to mine. He's got his usual obnoxious grin on his ruggedly handsome face.

I cross my arms over my chest and set my jaw as I give my brother a hard look.

"Liam, back the fuck off. I don't need to live with you to get out of my slump."

"Kind of do, man." Murph nods seriously, his overgrown dark hair falling into his eyes.

"We've all got superstitions, right?" Dean says, his dark eyes serious. "Most athletes do. Yours is to have a roommate and make sure you stay the hell away from relationships."

Murph adds, "So how do you manage? Same way I do— you fuck on the regular. You're doing that part just fine. But the first one? Clearly, you need a new roommate." He turns to Liam. "You left him high and dry."

Liam shakes his head. "Wasn't meant that way. He swore

he had a new housemate lined up. How was I to know he'd lied?"

"I didn't want you changing your plans for me," I say stubbornly. "I did have someone lined up. But he bailed at the last minute."

"Well, I've got a kid at home—and a wife," Liam says. "And you, Dean, and Murph have got what? Another weekend picking up the flavor of the month?"

I look into my older brother's narrowed green eyes. Sometimes, it's like looking in the mirror. But I'd never tell him that.

"You were just like us until Cathy got pregnant and you two decided to make a go of it," I say, giving it right back to him.

Liam's jaw turns to stone, and he runs his hand through the same dark wavy hair we can both thank our late father for.

"Watch it, little brother," he growls.

I tug at my own hair that's plastered to my head from sweat. "I'm happy for you; don't misunderstand me." I raise my hands in a surrender gesture. "I'm just saying—don't judge me because a part of you still wants to be free and easy."

And...I've touched a nerve.

"I love my kid, okay?" Liam's face is suddenly inches from mine. "And I love my wife. Just because the only girl you ever loved left town..."

I push him into the lockers. He may be older than me, but I've got three inches and twenty pounds on him. Being the tallest in the family comes in handy when you're the youngest of four boys.

"Jesus, Hunt," Liam says as I hold him hostage. "I'm sorry, okay? Winter just pushes all your buttons. She always did."

I press Liam harder against the lockers and pin his arm behind his back. "You better quit talking, big brother."

As usual, he doesn't listen. "Why don't you move on and find a nice girl to settle down with?" he says. "Then you'd have a permanent roommate and wouldn't be screwing up our playoff hopes."

At his last words, I still. "You're clearly not listening. I don't do relationships." Relationships are inherently messy, and I need to put all my focus on my career.

"Hey!" Coach Jones steps into our space and separates me from Liam. "Ease up, Storms. There's media around. You two brothers want to go somewhere private so you can beat the shit out of each other like you're kids again? No problem. But not here. Not when you're with the team."

Coach Jones may not have played in the pros, but he was a star college player, and he's still in excellent shape. He has no problem shoving Liam and me apart, nor any hesitation in giving us both a lethal staredown.

I back off, apologize to Coach, and grab my towel. I peel off the rest of my padding and uniform, wrap the towel around my waist, and head for the showers.

Murph and Dean catch up to me.

"Let's get drinks after this," Murph suggests. "Blow off some steam."

"Can't," I say. "I've got to remedy my living situation, remember?"

"You have a plan?" He raises one dark, bushy eyebrow in surprise.

"Sure I do. I have a pet sitter moving in to care for my cat. I'm gone so much I was paying through the nose for last-minute care by strangers I don't trust to do a good job, and I hate leaving her at a kennel. So, this will take care of two of my problems. Plus, I've got a late night planned with Deb."

"So, you'll get yourself a housemate in the form of a pet sitter, which also resolves your cat care problem." Murph holds up a finger. "And you've got plans with your on and off fuck buddy." He holds up a second finger. "Those two things should kill the slump, right?"

"Right." They better, or I could lose my place on the first line. And worse, we could miss the playoffs altogether. I've worked too damn hard for that to happen.

"Who's the pet sitter?" Dean asks.

I shrug. "Someone who knows the French Quarter. She used to live in New Orleans years ago. I asked for an older lady who won't be impressed by my profession, preferably someone who doesn't follow hockey at all. The agent told me she had it handled, and she's making sure the woman signs an NDA."

"Huh. A chick. Well, as long as you don't fuck her, right?" Dean says. "That will just complicate things."

"I'm not interested in screwing around with a live-in. You guys know that."

Murph shoots me a warning look. "And I know you, Hunt. Just remember, a roommate, even if she's hot, is off-limits."

Chapter 2
Winter

From the backseat of the taxi, I stare out the dirty window at the city lights as the driver weaves his way through New Orleans.

He doesn't drive as crazy fast as the cab drivers in Manhattan, but my stomach's queasy anyway. Must be that fast food I picked up when I got off the plane nearly an hour ago.

I shake my head at myself. Who am I kidding?

My stomach's queasy because of where I'm headed.

Home.

The place I swore I'd never return—New Orleans, Louisiana—where all I ever talked about when I lived here was getting out. Even if I'm only here temporarily, it still feels too long.

In just a few minutes, I'll pay the driver and step out into the heart of New Orleans—the French Quarter. I'll inhale the thick, humid air that reminds me so much of my childhood, air that always maintains a hint of the nearby Mississippi River. I can't deny I've missed the south, but the humidity does nothing good for my hair.

My phone rings just as the driver veers right sharply, and I brace myself to avoid slamming my head against the window.

"Hello, bestie," I say as I answer.

"Yay, you answered! That must mean you've landed!" Peyton's cheery voice comes through the receiver clearly.

I swallow hard, wishing I felt a hundredth as happy as she does living here. Peyton Black has the perfect set-up—she and her boyfriend, Scott, travel the country for months at a time in their motorcoach, and they also spend time visiting his family in Europe. With her business and her parents and brother in New Orleans, Peyton has the wings and the roots, which is all I ever wanted.

"That's right. I've landed," I say, trying to sound positive.

"Oh, sugar, you're miserable already," she says in concern.

The driver winds through the streets of the French Quarter, and I glance around with interest. It may be nighttime, but the Quarter never sleeps, and people are bustling about the curved streets. The pet sitting job that I applied for is right near here, which was one of the things that drew me to the position. I grew up wishing I could walk around the city at leisure, and this will give me the chance.

"How did your last audition go? The one for the lead on the new Broadway show?" Peyton asks me.

"Um..." I pause. "Not great. It was super competitive."

I don't tell her I bombed that audition, much like the one before, and that was the impetus for my manager insisting I take a few months' break and leave town.

"Your voice is shot, Winter," Pat said. "And you're not the same.

*Get out of the city for the spring and summer, and come back in the
fall for audition season."*

"But I can't miss any time here," I protested. *We had just met for
coffee around the corner from Times Square where Pat delivered the
bad news about my latest failed audition.* "I just got my big break.
That's why I'm getting all these calls. You know that."

*We both knew that one more blown audition might cement my
reputation as a one-hit-wonder. But Pat was kind enough not to say
anything. He just patted my shoulder and told me he'd stay in touch.
And then he walked away, leaving me standing on the sidewalk with
a half-empty cup of coffee and a nearly-finished career.*

"I'm sorry, sugar. Let Scott and me take you out tonight,"
Peyton says, bringing me out of my thoughts. "We'll meet up
with the others and go to the Riverway, not fancy like you
and your big-star self are used to with all those Manhattan
clubs, but it'll still be fun."

"That sounds great," I say. "But..." I hesitate and cut
myself off.

But Peyton's not one of my oldest friends for nothing.
"Hunter won't be there," she promises. "Well, I can't swear
that he won't be out and about, but everyone knows better
than to invite him to come with us when you're going to be
there."

I exhale as the cab comes to a stop outside a stand-alone
residence.

"But you do know you're going to have to see him sometime," she says gently. "I mean, I know you're returning to
New York, but you'll be here for a while, and the Storm
brothers are kind of a big deal around here. Especially once
the ice hockey team came to town, and Liam and Hunt
became its two biggest stars."

"It was easier when he played hockey elsewhere," I
murmur. "I could come home and know he wouldn't be
around. But now that he's here..."

"I get it." Peyton's voice softens. "But he's definitely here now. And he's pretty much impossible to ignore. You'll see the billboards of the team around the city, and his handsome face is plastered on all of them."

"Have you gone out with him at all?" I never ask her about the boy from my past, but I'd rather know in advance than be surprised later.

"A few times," she says. "My brother's seen him a bunch. And not just at his games." She pauses. "Hunter's party side hasn't exactly let up since you left."

"I'm sure it hasn't. I know I'll have to deal with him eventually. I just need a little time to get my feet down first."

I don't want to admit that seeing Hunter Storm again is the hardest part about returning to New Orleans.

I pay the driver and grab my one small suitcase. The rest of my stuff will be delivered to my parents' house tomorrow, so I'm traveling light. At least I don't have to live with my parents. I'll see them plenty, but the idea of moving back into my childhood bedroom is a bit too much.

I look up at the house before me curiously.

It's freshly painted in white with blue trim and is much better taken care of than I'd expected it to be. I had assumed it would have a barely lived-in feel, because the agent I spoke with explained how the owners are rarely home, but that they don't like to move their cat every time they leave on business. She said the owners are a young couple with a baby and that the man's line of work is rather "unconventional," but she didn't elaborate. And I didn't ask. This is New Orleans—unconventional could mean literally anything.

It's a two-story, townhouse-style home with a cute front porch and upper balcony. Being in the city, it's right next to the neighboring homes, but it has a driveway that leads into the back of the lot, and the entire property has a warm, homey feeling. And the location can't be beat. It's on a quiet side street only a block from Jackson Square.

The agent from the pet sitting service told me the owners would be home to meet me and show me around the place, so I climb the front steps. Catching sight of the sign that reads *Come inside porch to find doorbell*, I push through the screen door and step inside the porch, and that's when I come face to furry face with a handsome, orange-striped cat sitting on a porch swing and looking up at me with interest. I go to give it a quick pat.

"You're a sweetheart," I murmur into the kitty's long fur. "I could definitely take care of you."

The enclosed screen makes more sense now—it's a perfect space for a cat to hang out.

Before I can press the doorbell, I hear the door to the house open, and I straighten up. The wooden door opens outward, and it stands between me and the owner of the house, so I take the few steps around.

And...I suck back my gasp at who's standing in the doorway.

Holy. Shit.

For the first time in ten years, I stare up into the deep green eyes of Hunter Storm.

I immediately start shaking. I don't know if he notices. He seems a little preoccupied staring at my breasts.

He's so...masculine. His eyes are greener than I remembered. His dark, wavy hair's a little more tamed except for one lock that still falls over his forehead. His jaw is set and strong.

And Jesus, he's built. I get that he's a professional athlete, but wow...he's grown up nice. He's all man now.

I watch the muscles in Hunter's forearm flex as he braces his arm against the door. The urging to touch him is too strong, too scary. But God, how I want to.

I picked up the phone to call him a thousand times over the last ten years—when I blew my first audition and was sitting on the steps of my dorm room at NYU, crying my eyes out; when I broke up with three guys in a week because none of them made me feel a millionth of what I felt when I was with him; when I found out backstage I had to replace the lead of Seasonal Bliss and was certain I was going to throw up from terror. And of course, the last time I almost called him when my world was falling apart.

I always dialed his number but then hung up before he answered. And now, he's standing right in front of me.

Holy. Shit.

Chapter 3

Hunter

I open the door to let Theo inside.

Then someone steps around the corner into the doorway.

I suck in a breath as my world tips on its axis like it hasn't done in ten years.

Winter Princess Allen.

Her mouth drops open, and we stare at each other in silence.

"You're supposed to be my new boss," she finally says, immediately reaching for the spaghetti straps of her tank top, straps that have fallen off her shoulders, exposing creamy skin underneath.

I don't speak or move at first. I just take her in for a long minute—

Same chest-length black hair that I used to bury my fingers in; bewitching red pout that could swear like a sailor; and almond-shaped blue eyes that saw right through me like nobody else ever could.

Her pink frilly skirt is short enough that I can see the scar on her mid-thigh she got when she slipped in the lake and cut herself on a rock. The thin fabric of her top hides absolutely nothing, and her nipples are poking against the fabric, practically daring me to touch them. Her feet are in open-toed sandals, as usual, and her toenails are painted pink. Cotton candy pink, I think she used to correct me.

Winter looks as startled to see me as I am her.

"How'd you know where I live?" I say in a far-more accusing tone than I meant.

She furrows her eyebrows. "I don't know where you live. I'm here for the couple needing a pet sitter. *Shit*. Did I get the address wrong?"

She starts flipping through her phone.

Crap. I reach out and catch her wrist. "Don't bother. This is the right place."

Her eyes widen.

"You're the couple with the cat? The agency said the man travels a lot."

I gesture to the New Orleans Fire sweatshirt I'm wearing. "Road trip next week."

She sighs. "Oh Lord."

Oh Lord is right. I raise an eyebrow at her. "So you want a tour of the place?"

She looks at me like I'm nuts. "Right. Like you and I could live together peaceably. No, I'll just be on my way. My parents will be thrilled to see me, anyway. You know my father—always convinced the square is filled with murderers."

But after seeing Winter again for the first time in years, I'm not about to let her go that easily.

"You already came all this way." I step out onto the porch, and she inhales. "Do you want to come in? Or are you afraid you won't be able to control yourself if you get too close to me?"

She covers with a forced smile. "Did you know I was coming home?"

My short laugh cuts through the bullshit, and she blushes.

No man could make Winter blush but me. No one else could get through that layer of superiority her mother trained her in so well.

"Yeah, and I made sure to hire you. Because we ended things so well the last time." I try to say it jokingly, but the pain between us lingers.

One thing Winter and I always know how to do is fight. Ever since we were kids, we would get each other going. When we were young, those fights ended in making up with ice cream cones by the lake, and when we got older...let's just say a good fight between Winter and me finished in an even hotter make-out session.

She bites her lip like she knows what I'm thinking.

I watch her gather herself, put on her polite face, and nod. "Pardon my manners. I left Manhattan before dawn, so I didn't get a proper night's sleep."

But I can't let go of the thought nagging at me. "So why are you home, Winter? I figured a big Broadway star like you would be too busy these days to visit Louisiana. You just decided to come home for a while?"

She hesitates, and I can tell she's debating whether to tell a white lie or go for the truth.

When she exhales heavily and purses her lips, I know she's about to tell me the truth cloaked in some kind of a white lie.

"I hurt my vocal cords performing," she says in a voice so sad I nearly reach for her. "My manager sent me home. So, no more Broadway auditions until the fall."

I'm not sure which of the above was a lie, or maybe she simply omitted something. Either way, she didn't give me the whole story. But I'm not about to call her out on it right now. She's clearly in some kind of pain, and the last thing she needs is me being a dick.

"I'm sorry," I say gruffly.

"Thank you."

Ten seconds of us assessing each other in silence.

Yep. The chemistry's still there. Winter Allen can still rev me up like no other woman. And she's still off-limits—she was never meant to stay with me. She had her Broadway dreams to pursue, and hell if I was going to be the asshole to hold her back.

And I had my own dreams. Since we were kids, my three brothers and I were laser-focused on ice hockey. Sounds absolutely nuts to have a hockey dream in a southern city that, honest to God, didn't always have an ice hockey rink, but we caught hockey fever from watching the college and pro games on TV with our dad. He made sure we could go to camps every summer, and we travelled to Baton Rouge to play in a local club league that's since defunct.

Somehow, all four of us made the pros.

But my other dream—the one that involved Winter—apparently wasn't meant to be.

It's not like she and I ever even dated. We were...undefined. We weren't quite friends, and we weren't quite lovers—we were everything and nothing to each other, all at once.

So, I supported her Broadway dreams, and she supported my hockey ones. She'd leave town frequently to study in Manhattan, and I'd be gone in the summers for weeks at a time, practicing hockey. Somehow, our dual obsessive natures matched up. Our chemistry was nuclear, and no one could get my attention like she could.

But we were too singularly focused on our goals to have room for a real relationship. And when Winter moved to New York right after high school graduation as planned, to attend college and major in performing arts with her eye on Broadway, I stuck with my plan to attend college locally and throw all my energy into getting drafted.

She and I drifted apart like people do when they don't see

each other for years. To get through it, I put up a wall and firmly shut the door on keeping in touch.

But I was young and stubborn then. Now I'm older and slightly less obstinate.

"I've kept tabs on you, you know."

Winter's lips part. "You have?"

I can't believe I just revealed my hand, but no sense in holding back now. "I have." I look her right in the eyes when I say, "I'm fucking proud of you, Princess. You've done good."

The polite expression on her face eases, and she says, "Thank you, Hunt. That means a lot. And just so you know— I watch as many of your games as I can on TV. No matter whether you've been in Phoenix or New Orleans, I cheer for your team."

This surprises me. Winter always supported me unconditionally, but we ended in a fight...probably the only way we could say goodbye without it killing either of us.

"You cheered for the Phoenix Hawks?" I tease her.

"I cheered for *you*, Hunt. Wherever you were playing. I'm so proud of you, too."

"Thanks." I clear my throat, desperate to get rid of the emotion suddenly clogging it. "So you applied for this pet sitting job to avoid living at the Allen Jail?"

She breaks form at my joke, and a beautiful smile fills her face. That one dimple on her left cheek was always my undoing.

"Pretty much. But the rest of my time in New Orleans?" She holds up her hands. "Still figuring it out."

Something doesn't add up.

"What about your lead role in Seasonal Bliss? That must have opened a lot of doors, huh?"

She shifts from one foot to the other and looks past me out the window.

"Um...I've had issues auditioning. I've screwed up my last few."

I'm stumped. How could Winter be blowing her big break? She always relished the pressure; the bigger the spotlight, the brighter she shined.

But she clearly doesn't want to talk about it.

"Well, pet sitting is a fun gig too. Could teach you a few things in case you ever have to act alongside a cat."

Her smile doesn't reach her eyes. "Right."

I inhale.

I could stand here and talk to Winter forever. She's mesmerizing and fascinating and as complex and beautiful as she always was. But I can't look for something in a woman who's only here for six months max.

I open the door wide. "Come on. I'll show you around the house. No one knows better than I do the torture you're gonna be in for if you live with your parents while you're here."

Her mouth opens and then closes. I can practically see the wheels churning in her mind.

"The city's crowded, Winter. And not everyone who advertises for a pet sitter should be trusted."

She inhales so sharply I hear it catch in her throat.

"You okay?" I ask her.

"Yes," she stammers. "Fine. But I don't think you and I are good housemates material."

"Maybe not, but the chances of finding a safe place for rent this short notice is nil. Plus, you get a twofer—me and Theo here." I gesture to the cat, who's watching us both closely.

"What about your..." She almost seems to force the next word out. "Wife? Or is it girlfriend? And your..." Another pause before she says in nearly a whisper, "Baby?"

I cock my head. "I'm not following. It's just me here, Win.

That's why I need someone to look after Theo when I'm away."

She exhales. "The agency told me you had a family—and I *know* she mentioned a baby."

I hold up my hands. "I ain't got no baby, darlin'. Don't you think Peyton or Ash would have mentioned that to you?"

She shakes her head. "Outside of hockey, I ask my friends not to relay any personal information about you."

Ouch. "Well, I'm not a daddy. The agency must have gotten their information mixed up. I told them my brother moved out of here because he had a baby and got married. In that order."

Her eyes soften. "Which brother?"

"Liam. Max and Jared are still playing hockey for the Montana Wild Kings."

"That's right. Well, congratulations to Liam." Winter reaches over to pet Theo. "So he and Cathy stayed together, huh?"

"Yeah. When Cathy got pregnant, and then she gave birth and they tied the knot, this place just felt too small for them. Didn't want his little brother hanging around anymore while he changed diapers, I guess."

"Did you change any diapers?"

"Of course. I changed plenty of Lulu's diapers. She's my goddaughter and my favorite person in the world."

Winter's pretty pink lips part. "That's sweet, Hunt."

I touch Winter's sandaled foot with my bare one. "So you'll move in and take care of Theo here? You get your own suite."

She stares up at me. "Won't this kind of...suck? You and I haven't exactly been close lately. I can explain to the agency that I'm the one who turned the job down, and I'm sure they can find you someone else who's qualified."

I swallow hard. "I want you, Winter." *Always have.*

Our eyes lock. Whether or not she sees what's surely written all over my face—that nothing's changed since we were kids—I don't know.

Until she says gently, "You still can't live alone, Hunt?"

I look past her at Theo. "I've got Theo."

"You thought he'd be enough to kill the memories?" she asks in a strangled tone like she's reliving my father's murder as much as I am.

I force myself to meet her gaze. "I don't know. Maybe?"

She nods. "I get it. Okay. I'll give it a try."

I take Winter's hand in mine and lead her into the house.

"Will sure suck for me," I joke, "to have to see your Princess face every morning across the breakfast table."

She laughs.

Her hand still fits in mine. I should let it go, but I don't. Instead, I hold onto her all the way down the hallway and into the living room.

And she doesn't pull away.

We break apart awkwardly when she spins around to look at my place.

"The balcony must have a great view."

"You can use it whenever you like," I say.

"I can't believe this is yours." She holds my gaze. "Good for you."

"Thanks." My voice comes out gruff.

I show her through the rest of the house, trying not to sound like an ass when I point out the bathroom and kitchen I remodeled after Liam and I bought the place.

"This is amazing, Hunt." She stops in the middle of the kitchen. "It feels so warm."

I swallow, and the frustration of how well she fits in my house bubbles up in my throat and threatens to come out.

Instead, I turn on my heel and lead her up the short flight

of stairs. "And here's the guest suite. You've got your own bathroom."

She exclaims over the soaking tub and then wanders into the bedroom. She takes in the king-sized bed against the back wall and flanked by two windows. The walls are a pale green, and the only flaw in the space is a large dent in the door.

Winter looks right at it.

I start stammering something about Liam and his stupid temper, but she cuts me off with a smile.

"Let me guess—you two went at it one night after a few beers, and somebody missed a punch?"

The heat prickles the back of my neck and threatens to rise up into my face. "I'd never miss on a punch—you think I'd give up a chance to hit my brother?"

She throws back her head and laughs.

And I relax. I lean back against the door jam and smile at her. Those blue eyes of hers fix on mine like lasers until—

"So how did Cathy enjoy living here?" she asks, breaking the silence. "Can a woman handle this place, or will I run screaming back to my parents' house after the first night?"

"Darling, no woman runs screaming from me," I say slowly. "Although, you've always been the exception to that rule, haven't you?"

Her face flushes red, and she steps closer to me. She grabs two of the belt loops on my jeans and pulls me flush to her.

"I never ran from you, Hunter." Her breath is hot and smells like lemons.

"Pretty sure we both ran," I mutter as my hands go around her back and slide underneath her top.

I nearly lose my shit when my fingers land on the hot, soft, smooth skin of her back. The heat between her legs hits my sudden erection, and I swallow a groan. I rub my thumbs in circles over the small of her back, and she presses into me further.

"Are you seeing someone?" she asks in nearly a whisper. "Is there a woman I should know about who'll be staying here every night?"

Her blue eyes are flecked with violet, but the purple shade darkens to black as we stare at each other.

"No woman," I say in a rough voice. "You know I'm not into commitment."

I slowly drag one of my hands around her side. When I reach her stomach, she jumps backward so fast she bangs her head against the nearby lamp.

I widen my eyes. "What's wrong?"

She averts her gaze and reaches into her purse. When she produces her phone, I know she's intent on getting out of here before we finish this conversation. Well, that's not going to happen.

"Winter." I follow her out into the hallway. "Hey."

She calls for a cab before catching her lower lip between her teeth. I get a glimpse of the haunted look in her eyes before she ducks her head and charges for the front door.

"So I'll bring my stuff by tomorrow morning, okay?" she says over her shoulder. "I'll leave my suitcase here."

"Hey. Spoiled Southern Princess. Talk to me." I'm desperate to get her to slow down, and I use the name that pisses Winter off more than any other.

But even that doesn't get a rise out of her. She just gives me the smallest of smiles before darting out the door and down the walkway.

I step out onto the front porch. Within thirty seconds, I hear the squeal of tires, and I watch as the taxi she's jumped into disappears.

I stare down the empty street and shake my head.

Something just fucking happened. I didn't imagine it.

I run my hand over my face as I look down at Theo.

He looks back at me like he knows exactly what's going on and I'm the only idiot standing here in the dark.

I frown at him. "How the fuck do you know? You just met her. I've known her my whole damn life!"

Another haughty glance hits me before Theo starts cleaning his paws.

"Fine," I say to him. "So you're smarter than I am. But you're also a cat. So you have some limitations with women. I'm going to use all the tools at my disposal to figure out exactly what Winter Princess Allen's secrets are. I've got nothing better to do."

I've never had anything better to do than figure out Winter. And now that I'm going to be living with her in the same house, I can do just that.

I reach for my phone to cancel my date with Deb. As much as meeting up with her would no doubt help my tension, I'm no longer in the mood to see any woman but one.

To download the rest of **HUNTER**, a full-length stand-alone and book 1 in the Storm Brothers series, **CLICK HERE**!

ALSO BY MELISSA BELLE

Boston Boys

BOSTON BILLIONAIRE

BOSTON LOVE

BOSTON ESCAPE

BOSTON ROOMIE

BOSTON BAD BOY

BOSTON PLAYER

Wild Men

COLTON

DYLAN

AYDEN

JENSON

BRAYDEN

CAMERON

DECLAN

Wild Men Texas

WHISKEY GIRL

WARRIOR GIRL

WILD GIRL

Storm Brothers

HUNTER

MAX

JARED

LIAM

Bonus Wild Men Stories

WILD MAN (Colton and Sky prequel novella)

WILD VALENTINE (Ayden and Bella short story)

Sign up for Melissa's Newsletter to get a free story and to receive alerts and updates on upcoming book releases.

BONUS FREE WILD MEN STORY!

Ayden and Bella have everything they want...except one thing. Pick up **WILD VALENTINE** as a free bonus short story (complete with an HEA) **HERE**!

STAY UP TO DATE WITH MELISSA

Do you want to stay up to date on awesome sales, upcoming hot releases, and giveaways? Sign up for my VIP List and get a free story!

ABOUT THE AUTHOR

A USA Today Bestselling author, Melissa Belle is known for her contemporary romance style that's sweet, sexy, and smart. She writes hot, steamy romance with complex heroes and heroines. She spent years in the field of psychology before writing her first novel riding the train around Europe with her husband. Melissa likes cupcakes, road trips, and song-writing.

To receive an email when Melissa releases a new book, sign up for her VIP List!

www.melissabellebooks.com

www.ingramcontent.com/pod-product-compliance
Lightning Source LLC
Chambersburg PA
CBHW071344170626
46811CB00003B/983